ANNIE PEPPER

Sandra Savage

ISBN: 1500111678
ISBN-13: 978-1500111670

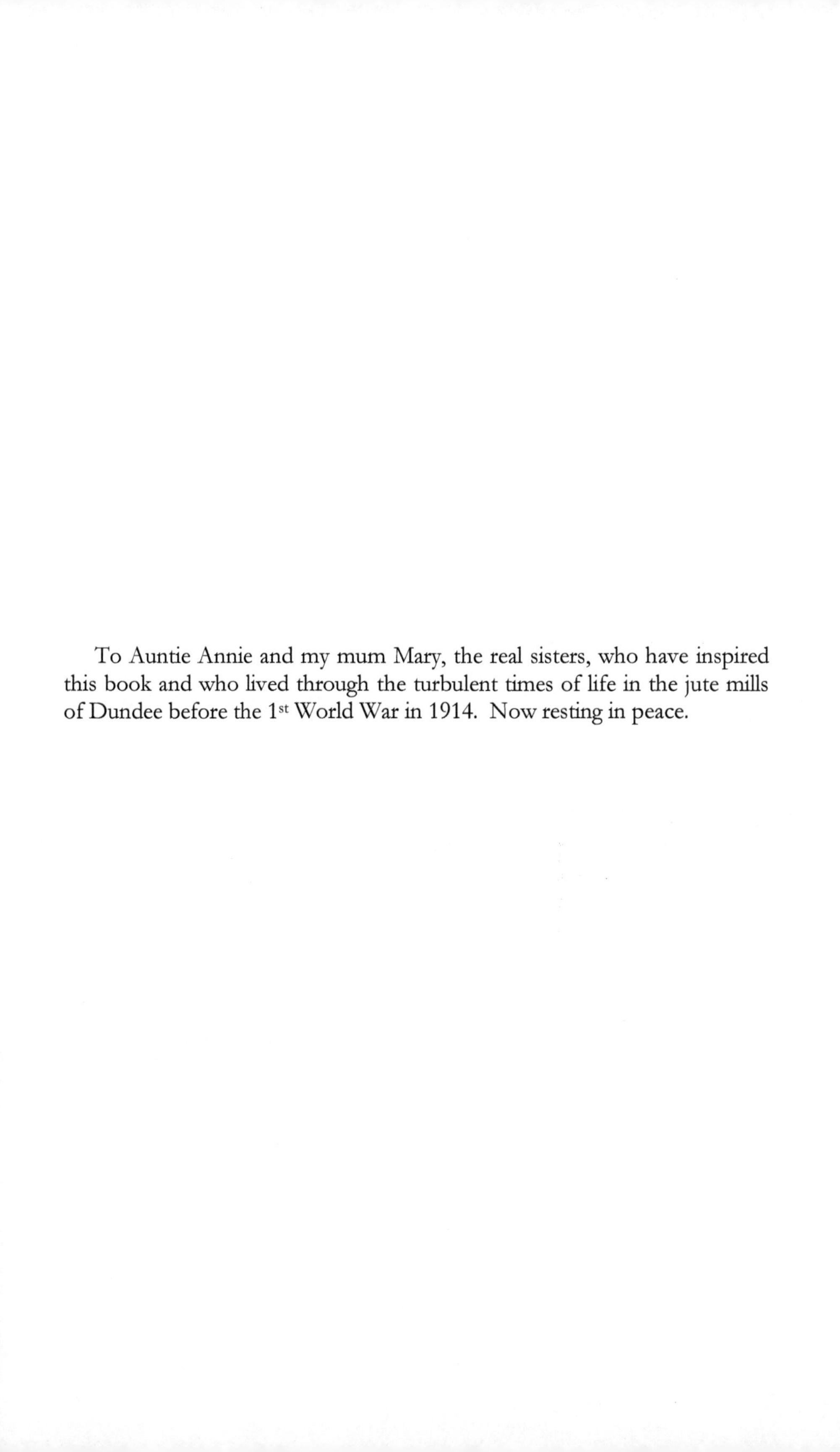

To Auntie Annie and my mum Mary, the real sisters, who have inspired this book and who lived through the turbulent times of life in the jute mills of Dundee before the 1st World War in 1914. Now resting in peace.

CONTENTS

CHAPTER 1

"Annie, Annie Pepper!" Her mother's soft Irish brogue drifted through the early morning air, disturbing Annie's daydream as she milked the cow. She loved milking, the rustle of the straw, the smells of the byre, earthy and familiar, and the sweet, warm milk frothing into the wooden bucket. She gathered up the folds of her course, brown skirt and wiped her hands down the front of her apron.

"Coming mammy," she called back.

Annie patted the velvet rump of Nell, and pushing back her brown hair, picked up the milk pail and started back to the house.

The chill of the morning touched her face and sounds of another ordinary day coming to life on the small Irish croft surrounded her. Annie pushed open the back door of the kitchen, where the warm glow of the peat fire lit the scene before her. Her mother was busying herself as usual, lifting the soda bread on to a wooden board to cool, while Annie's younger sister, Mary, stirred the pot of porridge on the black, iron range. The cat, drowsy from his nocturnal wanderings, lay stretched out on the rag rug in the corner.

Everything was as normal, except for one thing. Sitting at the scrubbed wooden table, his hands and face browned with the sun and a silver watch chain stretched across his black waistcoat, sat a man.

Annie's mother turned at the sound of her entrance.

"Annie, come away girl, there's someone you should meet."

Her face flushed with the heat of the range, she indicated the stranger, whose presence seemed to fill the kitchen as he stood up.

"This is your uncle's stepson, Billy Dawson. He's to be staying for a while, till the flax is gathered in."

Stepson! Annie had never seen him before in her life.

"Hello, Annie," said Billy, extending his hand towards her.

Annie rubbed her hand vigorously on her apron before shaking hands.

"Hello," she replied. His hand was strong and warm as it clasped hers and a smile flickered across his lips as he saw the blush of colour which had suddenly appeared on Annie's cheeks.

Billy Dawson was the tallest man she had ever laid eyes on. Well over six feet, older than her and with shoulders so broad and eyes so dark, it took her breath away.

"Billy's walked these twelve miles from Belfast to help us," her mother continued. "So you and your sister make sure you do your best to make him feel welcome."

"The porridge will be ready in a jiffy, Billy," piped up Mary, glancing at him with eyes that said more than they should in one so young.

'Forward madam,' thought Annie, who at twenty-four was some five years older than her flamboyant sister, although it seemed at times, in number of years only. 'How could she call him Billy, just like that!' she wondered, not for the first time taken aback by her sister's forthright manner. Such a nerve that girl had.

Annie filled a pitcher with the fresh milk and put it on the table as Mary ladled out bowls of steaming porridge.

"Tea, Billy?" Her mother motioned to his cup.

"Yes, thanks," Billy answered, his eyes moving around the female faces before him. Mrs Pepper's letter had reached him just in time, for he was set to leave Belfast to find work and had only delayed his plan out of respect for what he felt would have been his late stepfather's wish.

"I'm sorry to have arrived so early, Mrs Pepper," he apologised between spoonfuls of the oatmeal. "But the moon was so full last night, it was just like the middle of the day, and I knew by your letter that the sooner I got here, the better. I'm sorry about your man, Mrs Pepper," he continued, his voice dropping in respect. "To be taken like that, in his prime."

Annie's mother dipped her head and dabbed the corner of her eyes as tears threatened to fall.

A month ago, all had been well. The harvest was going to be good and everyone was looking forward to a happier winter with full stomachs. Then disaster had struck. Annie's father had been thrown from his horse during a summer storm and killed instantly. In desperation, Mrs Pepper had written to their only relative nearby, and that had been her late brother's stepson,

Billy, begging him to help with the flax gathering. To her relief, he had come.

She knew very little about him, except that his trade was weaving, he had no wife and he was Earnest's stepson. But by the fact that he had responded to her plea, it allowed her to believe that he was a good man, and she thanked God for his presence.

The porridge finished, they ate their soda bread and drank the strong tea, Annie wishing she had met Billy Dawson in her Sunday frock instead of the course skirt she had on. She rose from the table.

"I'll just get the pony and trap ready," she informed her mother. "We're needing a few things in the village and the quicker I get started, the sooner I'll be back to help with the pullin'."

"There's no hurry, Annie," cut in Mary, casting a sidelong glance at Billy's tall form. "I'll help Billy in the field, won't I Billy?"

Annie caught her breath. Quickly turning to her mother, she went on. "Was there anything special you were wanting, mammy?"

"No thanks, Annie," replied her mother. "But maybe Billy would be needing something."

For the second time that day, Annie felt herself blushing as Billy Dawson's eyes rested on her.

"No, there's nothing, Mrs Pepper, thanks all the same," he said, his eyes never moving from Annie's face. "But if I do think of anything, I'll be sure to let you know, Annie."

Annie forced a smile, as she felt her discomfort at Billy's gaze, intensify.

"I'll be off then," she hurried, almost knocking the milk jug over in her haste to leave the table. Then she was through the door and out into the cool air before anything more could be said.

By the time she had harnessed the pony to the trap, her breathing had steadied, and she began to scold herself for her foolishness.

"Anyone would think I'd never seen a man before," she chided herself. But even as she said it, she knew that she had never met anyone who had effected her the way Billy Dawson had.

The earth was soft under their feet as Billy and Mary made their way to the field to start the harvesting. The hired man was already there pulling the flax in great bunches and tying it into bundles ready to stack in the sun.

"I hope the weather holds," Mary called to Billy's back.

He didn't answer.

Her strong fingers began pulling the flax up by its roots.

"Mammy says you're a weaver in Belfast. Is that right, Billy?"

Still no answer.

Huffed at his lack of response, Mary bent to her task and the sun was high in the sky before Billy spoke.

"We'll stop now," he announced. "Some tea would be in order, I think."

Mary was glad of the break. She wished now that Annie would hurry back, so she could ease up. Keeping up with Billy Dawson was hard work, and not nearly as interesting as she had hoped.

They headed back to the house in silence. At 34, Billy knew about women, having bedded many a wench in his time and he knew Mary would be no exception, if that was his desire, but Billy's thoughts dwelt on Annie. There was something about Annie that disturbed him, maybe her innocence, or her openness, certainly not her looks. Fair she was, but not a beauty like her sister.

He pushed open the kitchen door and shook her image from his thoughts.

Mrs Pepper had the kettle boiling and soon they were gulping down the warm brew. Billy's shirt was opened to the waist and Mary could see the dark hair that covered his chest and stomach, and the glistening beads of sweat on his neck. She watched in silence as the muscles moved under the skin of his arm with each drink of tea he took, and wondered at his strength. The door opened and Annie entered, her arms clutching a sack of flour which she dumped on the floor by the window.

"Ah, Annie." Her mother bustled towards her. "Did you remember the sugar now?"

"Yes mammy, it's in the trap. I'll fetch it in a minute."

Billy Dawson stood up. "Let me. Here, have some tea, you look as though you need it."

Annie sat down with a bump, taken unaware by Billy's offer.

"Thanks… Billy." There, she'd said his name. A smile crossed his face.

"It's no trouble, Annie, no trouble at all."

Mary's voice cut through the moment. "Maybe," she began, emphasising the word, "when you've finished your tea, of course, you'd be good enough to lend a hand with the gathering. Seeing as how I've been working my fingers to the bone all morning while you've been swanning around the village."

Annie started at the harshness of Mary's tone. "Of course I'll help," she replied. "Don't I always?"

Mary pushed back her chair. "I'll get back to work then," she stated. "Ask Billy to bring some more baling twine with him." And without a backward glance, she was gone.

"What's the matter with that girl?" her mother asked, more to herself.

"It's high time she was married, that one. She needs a man to keep her in hand."

Annie began to colour. As the eldest, she should be the first to marry and it always hurt her that her mother seemed to overlook the fact. Or maybe it was that she thought nobody would want her now, not at her age. 'An old maid,' she thought. 'That's what'll become of me.'

She pushed the thought from her head and drank her tea.

"There's your sugar, Mrs Pepper." Billy's voice filled the kitchen. "I'll get back to work now."

"Billy." His name came easier this time. "Could you take some more baling twine with you? Mary says it's finished."

She ran to the kitchen dresser, pulled out a hank from the drawer, and handed it to him.

"Will you walk back to the field with me?" he asked, taking the string and pushing it into his shirt.

His eyes looked darker than ever and seemed to bore into Annie as he spoke.

Her voice came out in a whisper. "I'll just get my apron."

They walked to the field in silence, there seeming to be no need for words. The birds sang and the sound of her long skirt brushing the grass was like music to her ears as she strove to keep up with Billy's long strides. Annie had never felt so happy.

By the end of that first day, they were all exhausted. Harvesting the flax was back-breaking. Pulling the stems up by the root to get the maximum length of fibre was hard on the arms. It would get easier as they got used to it, but the first day of harvesting was killing.

"You're a hard worker, Annie," Billy commented as they ate the evening meal which Mrs Pepper had prepared. "And you too, Mary," he added. "Your daddy would've been proud of the pair of you. God rest his soul."

Mary's eyes lit up. So, he had noticed how hard she had worked after all.

"And I can play the banjo too." Mary beamed at him, like a little girl, eager to please. "Would you like to hear me?"

Billy laughed. "Not tonight, Mary, thanks all the same and, if you don't mind, Mrs Pepper, I think I'll turn in. We've an early start tomorrow and I'm fair whacked."

"Of course you are, Billy," Mrs Pepper agreed sympathetically. "Now don't bother Billy with that silly banjo of yours, Mary, can't you see he's had a hard enough day?"

Hurt at her mother's belittling of her musical skill in front of Billy, Mary retorted angrily, "It's not a silly banjo."

"Another night, Mary," soothed Annie, attempting to calm her sister.

Mary swung round to face her. "And you can just shut up for a start, you're just jealous, so you are." And with that, Mary flounced out of the room, banging the door behind her.

"Well!" exclaimed Annie's mother into the silent shock that followed. "I never did."

Flustered, she turned to Billy. "I'm sorry Billy," she apologised. "I think she's just overtired. I'm sure she'll be ashamed of herself in the morning."

Billy stood up, finishing his tea as he did so. "No need to apologise, Mrs Pepper, don't give it a second thought. It's been a long day." He bowed his head to Annie and her mother. "I'll say goodnight to you both."

Annie stared at her hands. What had gotten into Mary? Twice in one day she'd lost her temper. And she wasn't jealous of her banjo playing, to be sure she wasn't. It was all very confusing.

Mary's humour seemed to have improved by the following morning and, at her mother's insistence, she apologised meekly to Billy. Annie breathed a sigh of relief. She hated it when Mary was moody and, particularly now, she didn't want anything or anyone to spoil the inner glow of happiness which had developed since Billy's arrival.

The weather held, and all that week, Annie, Mary and Billy bent to the back-breaking task of gathering in the flax. There was no time for small talk, let alone getting to know Billy better and Annie had to content herself with stolen glances at his form as he worked and the pleasure of walking beside him on their way back to the house.

It was Mary who asked the question, quite unwittingly, that brought an answer from Billy which made Annie's heart jerk in her chest.

"When're you goin' back to Belfast then, Billy?" she asked.

"I'm not going back to Belfast," came the short reply.

Annie almost stumbled over a tussock of grass in her surprise. Could it be possible that he was looking to stay around a bit longer? Annie held her breath.

"You're not?" quizzed Mary further.

Although Mary was asking the question, Billy answered to Annie.

"No," he replied quietly. "As soon as I'm done here, I'm off over the water to Scotland."

Mary's voice babbled on. "What on earth would you be wanting to go there for, Billy?"

Annie could hold his gaze no longer and started to twist the hanks of twine over her arm into ever-tighter loops.

"For work. I'm told there's this new yarn, called jute, that they bring over from India and they've a desperate shortage of weavers to work it. The flax is dying out here, and there's nothing to keep me in Ireland."

Annie felt she would choke with disappointment. Going away, to Scotland. Her mind raced on. Never to see him again. Already it seemed almost too much to bear.

"Are you alright, Annie?" Billy's voice sounded softly in her ear, and she could feel his hand rest gently on her shoulder.

She looked up at him, but it was no use. She couldn't speak, but instead broke away and ran the full length of the field to the house, never looking back. She ran past her startled mother feeding the chickens in the yard, through the kitchen and up into the attic bedroom she shared with Mary, slamming the door shut and sliding the bolt. The tears rushed out of her in great sobs till she felt her heart would break.

"Annie!" it was her mother's voice at the door. "Are you alright, Annie… ? What's the matter?"

Annie pulled the pillow over the face to muffle the sound of her hurt.

"Annie," her mother's voice came again, this time more urgently. "Let me in girl, let me in."

Annie struggled to regain her control. "I'm alright, mammy," she managed to call out in a tight voice. "I'm just needing to be alone for a little while, that's all."

There was silence for a moment while Mrs Pepper considered the answer, before walking away, muttering to herself.

Annie hugged the pillow to her stomach and rocked gently back and forward on the edge of her bed until peace, once more, returned to her confused and troubled spirit.

If Billy Dawson thought anything about Annie's strange behaviour, he didn't let it show and all during the evening meal, but steered the conversation to lighter things.

"Why don't you get out that banjo of yours, Mary?" he asked, as Mrs Pepper cleared the table and refilled the kettle. Mary's eyes lit up in delight.

"Would you really like to hear me, Billy?"

"To be sure I would. Why, it's just what I need to take away the toil of the day, Mary. Fetch it here."

Mary skipped from the room and returned moments later clutching her much-loved banjo and settled herself on the milking stool by the ingle-nook. She started to play, her clever hands plucking the strings till they were a blur of sound, which set the feet tapping despite the mood of their owners, and soon, even Annie, who thought she would never smile again, began to feel her mood lighten.

She looked at Billy. His hands were hooked into the pockets of his waistcoat as his eyes watched Mary play.

"Well done, girl," he called out spontaneously, after she had finished. "Good God, you'd shame the Devil himself with that playing." Mary flushed with pleasure, and Annie felt a twinge of jealousy form in her stomach, acutely aware that she had no accomplishments, neither musical nor anything else and her looks were not of the type that drove men wild with desire.

Her sister sparkled before her, making Billy laugh with her comical songs and flirting with him with her blue eyes that could beguile and charm at will.

Annie felt her mood darken again.

"I think I'll be off to bed," she announced abruptly amid the jollity. "Goodnight."

There was a moment's silence as she walked to the door. Then Billy's voice sounded in her ears. "Goodnight Annie," he called softly after her. "Sleep well."

How she wished she could turn around and run to him, telling him of the stirrings she felt in her heart for him, but instead she left the small kitchen, closing the door behind her.

That night, Annie wept again, but by morning, drained of emotion, she had come to a decision. Before Billy went to Scotland, she would tell him of her feelings, no matter how futile that may prove to be. And then there was Mary. She was beginning to resent her own little sister and she didn't want that.

Breakfast the following morning was a silent affair. Mary sat pale-faced and heavy-eyed while Billy took only enough time to swallow his tea and soda bread before heading for the field.

"Are you alright, Mary?" Mrs Pepper asked of her younger daughter, eyeing her with concern.

I'm fine, Mammy," Mary responded quickly, pushing her half-eaten bowl of porridge aside. "It was late before I got to sleep last night, that's all."

Mrs Pepper removed Mary's plate from the table and tipped its contents into the cat's dish.

"Well, if you will sit up half the night prattling on to Billy, it's only to be expected," her mother retorted. Annie felt a chill round her heart.

"And what on earth were you and Billy talking about till all hours?" she asked, trying to keep the anxiety out of her voice.

Mary met her eyes as she stood up, tossing her dark curls off her face.

"Wouldn't you like to know, Annie Pepper," she whispered secretively, leaning across the table to make sure Annie heard every word. "And don't you just wish it had been you."

Annie's face began to burn.

"*No*," Annie shouted back defensively. "I do *not* and before I get to boxing your ears for your impudence, I'll thank you to get your chores done and remember your place."

But Mary swept past her, leaving Annie feeling angry and hurt.

When she felt calmer, she made her way to the fields, ready for another day gathering the flax. It was almost all in now and she gauged that by the end of that week, Billy would be moving on. She kept as far away from him as possible, her mind thinking of first one way, and then another, to let him know how she felt, but the more she thought, the worse it all got. Finally, she gave up and just hoped that the fates would lend a hand in her time of need. 'Maybe if I pray,' she thought. 'Mother believes in the power of prayer, although it never seems to make her life any easier.'

The midday sun burned her neck and arms. It was the hottest day yet.

"An hour down by the stream amongst the coolness of the trees wouldn't be noticed," she told herself. Billy was at the other end of the field with the hired man. She could slip away just for a while.

The sound of the cool water as it sparkled over the stones was like a balm to her soul as she slipped off her heavy boots and dipped her feet into the water. Despite the heat of the day, it was icy cold, running over the calves of her legs and between her toes. The trees filtered the heat of the sun and made patterns on the grass and Annie closed her eyes and began to breathe in the stillness.

It was a beautiful place. She always felt at peace here. Her thoughts drifted between her father and Billy. 'Would they have liked one another?' she wondered. She missed her father, so strong, so much part of the land. Gone now. Annie felt tears begin to form and slowly spill over onto her cheeks.

"Why so sad, Annie?" Billy Dawson's voice whispered near her face.

Startled by the sound, Annie swung round to find him kneeling beside her. Instinctively, she pulled herself away, but his hand caught her arm.

"It's alright, Annie. I won't hurt you."

Annie felt the tears well, again.

"Is it your father you're grievin' for, Annie? Or is it, maybe, something else?" Annie hung her head, unable to look at him. She felt him move closer till her head was resting on his shoulder and his hand was gently stroking her hair.

"Let it go, Annie girl," Billy whispered. "Let it go."

She felt herself lean into him, as he drew her even closer. She could feel the heat of his body and her fingers found a resting place on his chest. The whole world seemed to be still as she lay there, Billy's arms somehow protecting her from all the hardship and hurt she had ever known.

"Annie," he whispered. "Are you feeling anything for me at all?"

The question startled her for it sounded as though it mattered to him.

"Yes, Billy," was all she managed to say.

His arms tightened around her. "You know I have to go soon… don't you?"

Annie shivered despite the heat of the day. "Yes, Billy."

There was silence and she tried to picture the manner of his going.

"Annie," he continued, never releasing the hold he had on her. "What I'm wondering is…" His hands stopped stroking her hair and held her head to his chest, as if he feared she would look up and see his face. "I've no right in the world to ask you this, Annie," he began. "And I'll understand if you say, no… but…" His hold was so tight around her now, that Annie could barely breathe. "What I'm saying is… when I go to Scotland… would you come with me?"

The question hung in the air as if suspended by an invisible thread. Annie's heart was pounding as her head tried to take in what Billy was asking.

"Go to Scotland," she repeated to herself, hardly daring to believe what was happening.

"I know this may seem sudden to you," he went on, trying to control the sudden shaking in his voice. "But since that first day I saw you, I've wanted you, Annie. Please say you'll come."

His lips had found hers and before she could answer him, he was kissing her again and again, each time with more intensity. His hands moved over her body, searching out her nakedness under the coarse material that clothed her. She did nothing to stop him. Not wanting to. She knew now for certain, this was the man she loved.

The sun was beginning to dip behind the rim of the hill before Billy spoke again.

"I was the first, wasn't I?" he asked, pleased and afraid at the same time.

She knew what he meant. "Yes."

Billy flinched, a shimmer of guilt touching his heart. "I'm sorry Annie. I didn't mean to do that to you… out of wedlock an' all."

"It's alright, Billy…" Annie took a deep breath. "I love you, you see, so it doesn't matter to me if the marriage comes second."

Billy's stomach tightened at the word marriage, as it always did. The very thought of being tied down filled him with dread. Love was one thing, but marriage, that was quite another. Billy sat up quickly, fastening his shirt and pulling on his waistcoat. "We'd best get back to the field." he muttered. "Mr O'Connor will be wondering where I am. I said I'd be back in an hour."

Annie scrambled to her feet as he walked up the bank, almost having to run to catch up with him. "When'll you tell Mammy, Billy, about our going to Scotland?" she asked between breaths.

"When I'm good and ready," he replied, never slowing his step nor turning to look at her. "And, don't you go saying anything till I am."

At the end of the day, they walked back to the house in silence as Annie's confusion deepened. "What's wrong Billy?" she asked eventually as they neared the house, unable to stand his seeming indifference any longer.

"Nothing's wrong, Annie," he answered, slowing his pace, resignation in his voice. "I just don't want your mother suspecting anything just now. It's going to be hard enough to tell her when the time comes, so just act normal and leave it to me, please."

Annie nodded. "Whatever you say, Billy."

He bent down and kissed her on the forehead, hating himself for his lust yet wanting to take her again. "Good."

CHAPTER 2

The next three days saw the finish of the flax, and Annie spent the time dreaming of what Scotland would be like and how they would live once she and Billy were married. Mary continued to avoid her and seemed to go more into herself, which wasn't like her at all.

Annie watched her mother too, conscious of the fact that she might never see her again, and began to worry how she and Mary would manage when she was gone. She had been so wrapped up in her new-found love that the thought of how they would cope without her never entered her head… till now.

It was late afternoon and her mother was busy mixing a batch of scones, when Annie decided to broach the subject.

"Mammy," she began. "I've been thinking about how things'll be for us now that father has gone… I mean, we've had Billy here for the gathering, but he'll be goin' soon, and how're we goin' to manage for next year's crop?" Annie's mother stopped mixing and wiped her flour-dusted hands on her apron.

"The short answer to that Annie girl is… I just don't know." She lifted her eyes heavenward. "It's in His hands now. We can't stay here much longer, you can be sure of that. It needs a man about to work this land, and anyway the landlord's already got another tenant lined up, so we're to be moving out soon, although where to, I don't…" Her voice trailed off and Annie watched her shoulders crumple under the weight of the unknown.

She led her mother to the chair by the fire and knelt beside her.

"It's alright, Mammy," Annie whispered. "Please don't worry…

something will turn up, I just know it." She tried to sound reassuring, but she now knew that, short of a miracle, they'd be homeless before the year was out.

'I must talk to Billy,' she decided. 'He'll know what to do.' She finished making the batch of scones and settled her mother with a cup of tea before going in search of him. She found him clearing out the byre and for a few minutes watched his strong body raking the straw and man-handling a fresh bale from the loft. They hadn't said much to one another since the day at the stream, but words hadn't been necessary. Billy would say what was to be said when the time was right. She was sure of that.

She crossed the yard towards him, and he turned at the sound of her approach. She could have sworn she law his eyes light up as he saw her, but almost instantly it was replaced by a dark shadow.

She spoke first. "I'm worried about Mammy, Billy," she began. "I've been talking to her about the future and… oh! Billy… I don't know what's going to become of her and Mary after we've gone."

Billy cupped her face in his hands and kissed her gently on the forehead. "Come with me Annie girl, down by the stream." He took her hand in his.

Without talking, they walked across the field and down the riverbank to the place where they had made love only a few days before.

"Now, tell me what's happened," Billy asked as they sat near the edge of the water on the soft grass.

"It's Mammy and Mary," Annie began, trying to keep her emotions in check. "What will happen to them when we've gone? Mammy says they won't be able to stay on the farm and there's no one to take them in. And, I'm scared Billy, scared for them and for us." Annie threw herself into his arms, her fingers clinging onto his shirt like a life raft.

Billy smoothed her hair, just like he'd done that first day and breathed a sigh of relief.

"Ssshhh, Annie," he soothed. "I know how it is. Haven't I been worried about the same thing myself, ever since I realised how things were between you and me. Sure to God your mother isn't getting any younger, and Mary's more than a handful." He pulled her closer to him, as if he felt she would see through his lies if she looked at him.

"What's to be done, Billy?" Annie whispered, anxiety and despair in her voice. "How can I go and leave them here?" Even as she formed the words, her heart stood still. For in her staying, it would mean her having to say goodbye to Billy and in her heart of hearts, she couldn't bear that.

"Don't say that Annie." Billy's voice sounded strained.

"But, what's to be done Billy?" Annie cried, the emptiness somewhere inside her increasing with every word, for she could see only unhappiness no matter what she did.

Billy's arm tightened around her. "Ssshhh, Annie love, ssshhh." They sat in silence for a long time, just holding one another, Annie hoping for a miracle to happen so they could be together without guilt.

"Perhaps, we're going to have to part," Billy said quietly, surprised at the emptiness the words brought to him. He didn't want marriage, never had, but the love of this woman was causing him to doubt his selfish existence.

Annie's heart froze.

The words seemed to paralyse her senses rendering her incapable of coherent thought.

She looked at him, searching his face for a denial of what he had just said. But there was none.

"I have to go to Scotland, Annie," he said urgently, dismissing the weakness from his mind. "I know there's work for me there. There's none left in Ireland." Annie's eyes filled with tears. She knew he was right, but riled against the fates for the truth of it.

"Your mother needs you Annie," Billy continued. "You know that. Mary isn't much help and with your father recently gone, it would break her heart to lose you too."

Tears flowed down Annie's face, unashamedly, as she sobbed her heart out for the pity of it all. Billy hated himself for her hurt. 'Is that all there is to me?' he asked himself. "Love them and leave them?' But he had no answers, only the need to leave this place as soon as he could.

When there were no more tears left to cry, Billy gently released her and helped her to her feet.

His brown eyes fixed on hers. "I can't ask you to come with me now Annie, not just now. But will you never forget me Annie, and know that I'll always love you."

The words seemed like a death knell in her ears. How could he say he loved her and not want to be with her? Annie didn't understand any of it.

She hung her head. "Yes, Billy," she answered. For she knew she never would forget him. She would always be his.

"Be brave, Annie," he continued. "I'll write to you as soon as I get to Scotland and we'll find a way to be together again, God willing, one day."

Annie's legs dragged her body up the riverbank and back to the house. They walked in silence, her wits unable to react, overwhelmed by the thought that Billy would be leaving soon and powerless to do anything to stop it happening.

Guilt ate at Billy as they walked back to the house. Annie was like a wounded fawn and it was he who caused the hurt. In a surge of remorse,

Billy suddenly stopped and pulled her towards him.

"Let's talk to your mother Annie, explain things," he announced, desperation in his voice. "Find a way."

Annie nodded silently, following him into the house, a small well of hope rising in her breast.

Mrs Pepper was raking the coals in the range, coaxing them back into life. She turned at the sound of their entering.

"Billy! Annie!" she exclaimed. "Come away in and sit yourselves down. There's tea in the pot."

"You've been a great help Billy lad. I don't know how we'd have got the flax in without you…"

Billy interrupted her flow. "Mrs Pepper, Annie and me… we'd like to talk to you."

Mrs Pepper's eyes levelled with his. "Oh, yes?" she queried, pouring the tea into their cups. "Well go on lad, I'm listening."

Billy took a deep breath. "Firstly, you should know that now the flax is in, I'll be leaving soon. I'm going to Scotland."

Annie's mother handed him his tea. "Well, I hope you'll be very happy, Billy, to be sure, you're a good man and a hard worker."

Annie glanced anxiously at her mother as Billy continued. "The thing is, Mrs Pepper… Annie and me… we've come to an understanding."

Mrs Pepper put down the teapot. "An understanding is it?" she repeated, sitting down in her chair. "And what might that mean?"

Billy's jaw tensed. "We love one another, Mrs Pepper," he stated firmly. "And we want to be married."

Annie's mother's face clouded. "Has Annie told you about the farm then, about how we're going to have to leave it before the winter sets in?"

Billy nodded.

"And has she told you that we've nowhere to go?"

"She's told me that too, Mrs Pepper."

"And now you say that she and you have this understanding." She struggled to her feet. "So you're going to take my daughter away from me now, are you?" Her voice was becoming higher, as the fear of what was happening, gripped her.

Annie's stomach tightened at her mother's distress. "No, Mammy," she shouted. "That's just what Billy's trying to say, although we love one another… I won't be going with him to Scotland, I can't, you see… and leave you and Mary like this." Her voice faded with the words.

There was another silence before Billy spoke again.

"Mrs Pepper. What I want to say is, if I can find a place and work for us, would you and Mary be willing to come too?"

Annie's breath quickened. Billy would do that for her. To be with her. She felt a great well of love wash over her. "Oh, Billy."

Mrs Pepper clasped her hands in front of her. "No" she replied simply, tears filling her eyes. "I've lived in Ireland all my life, and I'll die here, Billy Dawson." She turned to Annie. "And if you want to go traipsing off to Scotland on the promise of a man you hardly know, then that's up to you."

She pushed her chair back under the table and walked from the room, leaving Billy and Annie sitting there.

Annie felt herself crumble inside. The hope that had so quickly flared in her heart, just as quickly now vanished.

"Oh, Billy," she whispered, her heart breaking. "She won't come ever, will she?"

Billy's eyes darkened. "It doesn't look like it Annie, it doesn't look like it. I'll leave tomorrow," he stated woodenly, his eyes taking in every inch of Annie's form. "Let's get out of here," he said almost harshly. "If I have to leave you then let me love you before I go." He took her hand in his, the warmth of her body arousing him again. "I'll let you know where to come when the time's right, Annie," he said, almost believing it himself.

Annie nodded.

"See to your mother's needs, then come to me, Annie, with all your heart." That day they lay with each other by the stream till darkness fell.

"When you wake up tomorrow," Billy whispered. "I'll be gone." He pulled her tighter to him. "But don't cry Annie, know that I'll be waiting for you and longing for you to come to me."

Annie's voice sounded in her head, not like it belonged to her at all. "Yes, Billy," was all she could manage.

The next day, he was gone.

CHAPTER 3

Dundee was a hard-working town and Billy had never felt so alone in his life. Ireland seemed at the other end of the world and he clung to the warmth of Annie's memory despite himself. It wouldn't be so bad if she were his wife, he reasoned in the darkness of the tiny room where he lodged. At least he'd have a kindred spirit to come home to and not these Scottish women who seemed to speak a foreign language and whom he didn't understand, never mind desire. Wasn't it high time he married anyway, father some young, be a proper man?

Convinced now he was doing the right thing, Billy wrote to Annie.

He told her of Dundee and how he'd got work in one of the jute mills there. Baxter Brothers had made him an overseer almost immediately because of his experience of flax weaving, and he'd got lodgings in the house of a mill family who lived at a place called Dens Brae, a steep hill near the mill. He was already looking for something for both of them for when she could join him and hoped she was well.

It was three weeks later when Billy's letter arrived.

Down by the riverbank, where she could feel his presence, Annie opened it.

The letter seemed full of hope and Annie felt her spirits rise as she read it. "Thank you God," she whispered, as tears of happiness threatened to tumble from her eyes. "I know everything's going to be alright… I just know it." She carefully folded the letter and returned it to its envelope. She would sleep with it under her pillow tonight and dream of Billy.

Skipping and singing to herself, she ran back to the house, but her happiness was short-lived.

Annie's mother had received word from the big house that a new tenant would be moving in come October, only a month away, and that they had to clear their possessions out by the end of that month.

Mrs Pepper handed Annie the piece of paper. "Here, read it for yourself and then tell me what we're to do!" It was more a statement than a question and it felt, to Annie, that her mother had given up already and was now just awaiting the inevitable that would see the end of her.

She knelt beside her. "Oh, Mammy," she crooned, her voice fraught with concern. "I'll think of something, please don't worry. Mary and me will look after you." But her reassurances fell on deaf ears and it was all Annie could do to keep the anxiety from overwhelming herself, never mind finding an answer to their dilemma.

Another two weeks passed even more dismally than the previous three, when Annie realised she was pregnant. At first, she'd been scared, but as the days passed, the fear had left and the knowledge that Billy's child was inside her somehow strengthened her to deal with the depression that was forming all around her.

She watched her mother grow older by the minute as the days at the farm grew less, while Mary seemed to spend her time plucking aimlessly on the strings of her banjo or lying alone on her bed. There seemed no hope for Annie or her mother and sister as October turned and their last month on the farm began.

"I'm going to Belfast," announced Mary one day, out of the blue. "I'm tired of waiting around here to be thrown out. I'm told there's plenty of work there for a clever girl like me." She tossed her head defiantly and Annie felt both apprehensive and glad at the same time. It had been a while since Mary had shown any sign of her old spirit, but to go to Belfast, on her own!

Mrs Pepper too seemed to regain her fight. "You'll do no such thing my girl," she stated adamantly. "No daughter of mine is going to walk the streets of Belfast to be picked up by some heathen."

But Mary was ready for her. "And just how are you going to manage to stop me?" she demanded. "You may be able to rule Annie's life, but you'll never rule mine." And with that, Mary strode out of the kitchen and before the week was over, she had left the tiny farm and her family without a backward glance.

Part of Annie wished she had Mary's ability to put herself first, but then, she never had been like her sister.

Sometimes, she wondered if her mother had spoken to Mary as she had, deliberately, knowing if she objected to what Mary wanted to do, that's exactly what her wilful daughter would do.

"And what are you hanging around for Annie Pepper?" her mother had rounded on her one night after Mary had gone. "Isn't that man of yours waiting for you in Scotland. Waiting to make you happy?"

But Annie knew then what her mother was up to.

"Mammy." Annie knelt beside her. "Don't say these things to me."

The old woman's eyes filled with tears, as the strain of the last few weeks overwhelmed her.

"It's the end, Annie," she whispered. "For me anyway." She folded like a soft blanket into Annie's arms. "Just leave me here to die," she moaned. "Your dad's waiting for me."

Annie held her tightly. "You're not going to die, Mammy, not if I have anything to do with it." Annie took hold of both her hands. "Let's both go to Scotland," she begged. "Billy's working now, and he'll find a place for us. Come with me Mammy, please?"

The barriers that had been lowered were suddenly raised again. "I've told you before," stated Mrs Pepper, her voice shaking with emotion. "I'm not leaving Ireland… I'll die here."

Annie's heart sank. Her mother could be obstinate when she wanted, she knew that, but she also knew now, she would never leave Ireland.

The final week at the farm dragged on and the morning sickness was making Annie feel listless and weary. In desperation, she went to see Father Dominic, their Parish priest, but all he could do was arrange for them to be taken in at St Theresa's Poor House in Belfast. Annie prayed with all her heart and soul that, somehow, they would be spared this end, but her prayers remained unanswered and on a chill autumn morning on the last day of October, she packed their meagre belongings in two wooden boxes and steeled herself for their journey to Belfast and the Poor House.

She wrapped her father's watch and the silver brooch he had given her on her twenty-first birthday in a linen hankie and tucked it into the pocket of her skirt. She didn't want to lose the only two things which reminded her of her dad and, not for the first time, wished he was still with them.

At ten o'clock the hired man, Mr O'Connor, arrived with his small cart. He'd got a buyer for the little furniture that had been theirs, and this, along with the other bits and pieces, had realised three Guineas. Annie put the money in her skirt pocket and thanked him for his help.

"Could you take us to St Theresa's in Belfast Mr O'Connor? It's awful far for Mammy to walk, although I know she'd try…"

Mr O'Connor put his finger to his lips. "Hush now Annie. Of course I'll be taking you to Belfast. Isn't it the least I can do in memory of Mr Pepper?"

Annie smiled bravely and nodded.

She lifted their two boxes onto the back of the cart and helped her mother up beside them. Annie sat by Mr O'Connor, forcing back the tears.

St Theresa's was run by the Sisters of Mercy, and gave shelter to the destitute and Annie dreaded to think how they would survive it, especially her mother.

The cart rumbled away from the croft, down the track and onto the Belfast Road. The air was crisp and cold, and the autumn - usually a season Annie loved - went past unnoticed to her. Her thoughts were of the future and her babe, still to be born, and her mother worn out and dependent on her. She wondered too where Mary was. Perhaps she would find her in Belfast and they could be together again. She missed Mary with her fighting spirit and quick wit.

Mr O'Connor pulled on the reins, stopping the horse outside a grey brick wall with an iron gate set into it.

"We're here, Annie," he announced solemnly. "Is there anything else I can do for you and Mrs Pepper?"

Annie began unloading their boxes. "No thanks, Mr O'Connor. You've been more than kindness itself." Annie thought her mother would collapse as she helped her down from the cart.

"We're here, Mammy," she said, trying to sound optimistic. "It'll be alright now."

Annie's stomach tightened into a knot as a black-swathed nun approached the gate.

'Why do they have to look so cold?' she thought. Not like Father Dominic who had given her her first communion and who had comforted them when her father had passed on.

Without a word, the gate swung open.

Annie bade goodbye to Mr O'Connor and put her arm protectively around her mother's shoulders, giving her a gentle hug.

"Come on Mammy," she whispered encouragingly. "We've to follow the nun."

The inside was just as bleak as the outside and Annie shuddered at the stark wooden floorboards and cracked paintwork. There was a row of wooden beds along one wall and the nun stopped at the last two.

"These are yours," she said almost imperceptibly, then she was gone.

Annie pushed their two boxes below one of the tiny bunks and sat her mother down on the other. She took her worn hands in her own and looked into her eyes.

"Mammy." She spoke quietly. "We don't have to remain here, we can go to Scotland where Billy'll look after us. Won't you change your mind?"

Annie's eyes pleaded with her mother's. But the answer was still the same. Annie's shoulders slumped. It was no good. If even the reality of the poorhouse, with all its bleakness couldn't make her change her mind, nothing would.

That night, after she had settled her mother as comfortably as she could, Annie wrote to Billy. She told him where they were, and how her mother still wouldn't change her mind about leaving Ireland. All the hopelessness she felt inside poured out of her. She didn't tell Billy about their baby, for she knew he would come for her and they would be back in the same position as before. She looked across at her mother, lying fitfully sleeping, and her heart ached.

The baby had begun moving inside her and Annie felt a closeness to her unborn child that she never knew was possible. In all this misery, it was the only hope for the future she had. And it was part of Billy, her Billy, the only man she had ever loved and ever would love. Billy, whose love she so desperately needed now.

The next day, Annie posted her letter to Dundee and went into the streets of Belfast to look for work, but with the flax mills closing all around, work was scarce and poverty stood in huddles on every corner. Dejected and weary, she trudged back again that night to the depression of the Poor House.

The meagre meal that the Sisters provided consisted of boiled potatoes, soda bread and a mug of tea. Annie ate ravenously, but her mother picked at the food in front of her.

Annie eyed her worriedly. "Eat up Mammy," she urged. "You have to keep your strength up for when I get working and we can get a place out of here."

Her mother looked at her with empty, listless eyes. "I'll never leave this place, Annie," she muttered flatly and, sighing deeply, added, "Mark my words… never."

Annie shuddered. "Don't say things like that now, Mammy, or I'll be getting cross with you. You're as strong as a horse and don't I know it."

Mrs Pepper reached out her hand to her daughter and, clutching it shakily, shook her head. Annie searched for words which would reach into her mother's despair and turn it away, but could find none.

The days wore on, with no sign of work and never a ray of hope for the future. Each night, on her return, Annie would tell her mother of what they would do when she found work and how it would be alright soon, but Mrs Pepper seemed to be fading away before Annie's eyes and she seemed powerless to do anything to prevent it. Before many more days had passed, her mother fell into a deep sleep from which she never awoke.

The tears Annie had expected to fall didn't come just then. For it was a blessed release to both of them that her mother had passed on. The simple burial was paid for out of the money Mr O'Connor had got for their furniture, with only Annie, the priest and the grave digger there to mark her mother's passing. The Priest held her hand while the grave digger shovelled the earth over the coffin.

"Will you be alright," he asked quietly.

Annie nodded. "But I think I'll just stay here for a while, if you please."

The Priest smiled and squeezed her hand.

Alone beside the patch of fresh earth in the graveyard of the Poor House, Annie's tears came tumbling down her face for the pity of it all. She wept for her mother and father, her sister Mary, Billy and her unborn baby, but most of all, she wept for herself. She could count on the fingers of one hand the days of joy she had had, and most of these had been with Billy. She would go to Scotland now and there she would find the happiness that had been denied her.

Back at the Poor House, drained of all emotion, she mechanically packed her box. Her mother's few clothes she gave to the other women who had shared their dismal existence these last weeks. Haggard women, old before their time, left to survive or die at the whim of fate. She sat on the edge of the bed and started to write a letter to Billy and was lost in the writing of it, when a movement at her shoulder interrupted her thoughts.

It was one of the nuns. Silent and black. She handed Annie an envelope. Recognising Billy's handwriting immediately, her heart soared.

"Thank you," she said to the silent figure. "For bringing me this." Annie indicated the letter. "I'll be going soon," she continued. "To Scotland. Thank you for all you've done."

The nun nodded once, turned silently and left.

With trembling fingers, Annie prised open the fold of the envelope and smoothed the single sheet within.

'Dear Annie,' it read, 'I know times are hard for you just now, and I'm sorry it's gone that way for you and Mrs Pepper, but there's something I have to tell you. Mary's here.' Annie almost dropped the page in disbelief. Mary, in Scotland, but how… why? She read on.

'It's like this,' the letter continued. 'Mary and I are married.' The page froze in Annie's fingers. She re-read the line. 'Mary and I are married.'

She forced herself to read on.

'She's pregnant, Annie, with my child, and I have a duty to her. It wasn't meant to happen like this, but I cannot turn my back on my own child.'

The ending was cold and formal.

I hope you and your mother are well.
Goodbye,
Billy.

The page fell from Annie's lifeless fingers. Mary and Billy! It was as though time had stopped, it was as though her life had ended.

Annie sat there for a long time, her mind wandering where it would, tears running absently down her face and her eyes fixed on a shaft of pale sunlight billowing with dust, making patterns in the air. She felt nothing, no fear, no pain, no laughter, no hope.

'Do people die of broken hearts?' she wondered, not really caring. She wanted to die, right now, at that moment in time, alone in the Poor House, she wanted to die.

Just then, she felt her baby moving within her. A soft rippling movement. Her hands stroked her womb protectively. "I hear you little one," she whispered. "I hear you."

Annie lay down on the rough bed, pulled the blanket over her head as if to shut out the world and fell into an exhausted sleep.

CHAPTER 4

Mary tried to stir some life into the fire struggling to keep alight in the range. The two rooms she now shared with Billy, as his wife, were part of a tenement of flats, mostly housing mill workers, like Billy, from Baxters Mills. Their tenement home was accessed through a narrow close between the building and a small courtyard, where women hung their washing out to dry and where ragged children played with anything they could find to amuse themselves.

A gas lamp, which cast a shadowy glow at night, sat in a bracket half-way up a winding stairwell which led to a row of doors ranged along a stone platform.

Mary and Billy's home was another level above this and looked north towards Victoria Road from the kitchen and South over Todburn Lane and King Street from the backroom.

As she stirred the embers, Mary wondered how Annie had taken the news of her marriage to Billy. She hadn't meant things to turn out as they had, but that night with Billy, when she'd played the banjo for him, had aroused an urgency in her to gain his attention that had taken even her by surprise. She had flirted and fluttered around him like a wild moth, teasing him with her music and charming him with soft words. She had sensed Annie's feelings for Billy were strong and it had seemed to make her all the more determined to win his favour.

"Billy," she had murmured when they were both alone and he had tired of her banjo playing. "Let me take off your boots and wash your feet." Billy had laughed out loud, but obliged her good-naturedly, and had allowed her to remove his workboots and splash the warm water, which she had brought in an enamel basin, over his ankles and toes. She had rubbed the soap into the soles of his feet and he had smiled a relaxed smile as she began to dry them with a small towel.

As she did so, his hand had drifted over her hair and the air had become silent as Mary moved closer to his knee.

As if in slow motion her eyes had closed as she had covered his hand with her own and moved it to her cheek. Billy had felt himself lean into Mary as she pulled him to the floor beside her. There was to be no going back for her now. She had decided that when Annie had taken herself off to bed and she had felt a stab of jealousy as Billy had watched her go. She had determined, she would be the one to get his attention that night and, that night, Mary succeeded.

It wasn't the first time she had lain with a man - she and Mr O'Connor's son had done it in the nearby wood last summer - but Billy was different, Billy made love to her like a man.

When it was over, he had stared at her, almost in disbelief at what they had done.

"You must never speak of this to anyone," he'd cautioned her roughly. "Do you hear me Mary? No one." Unable to do anything else, Mary had nodded in agreement and during the following days and weeks till he left for Scotland, neither of them had mentioned that night again.

When she had realised she was pregnant, Mary had felt scared and sorry for herself all at once. She had found Billy's letter to Annie in its hiding place in their room and painstakingly copied down his address. She would let him know what he'd done to her and make him come back and marry her, but she soon realised that Annie would have something to say about that and decided to run away to Belfast instead, more out of fear and panic than common sense.

Mary was soon to realise her mistake. Work in Belfast was hard to find, as was a roof over her head, and for the first three days she had slept where she fell. Her courage and strength were almost gone when she was found huddled in a doorway in the early hours of a Sunday morning by a young woman, not any older than herself, in a Salvation Army uniform.

During the days that followed, Mary had been given warm clothing and food and encouraged by her benefactor, who was unaware of Mary's condition, to return home to her loved ones. But Mary knew this could never be, and grew more and more desperate in her plight as the search for work continued to prove fruitless and her pregnancy advanced.

The more desperate she got, the more her thoughts turned to anger at Billy for her condition, despite the fact that it was she who had engineered the fateful coupling. It was then she had decided to write to him. Her words were few, as she had not liked learning and writing was a struggle for her. 'I am having your child inside me,' she had said. 'Help me. Mary.'

She slowly printed the address of the Salvationist Home in Belfast and posted the letter.

Billy had been working fourteen hours a day at the mill to make enough money to send to Annie so she could join him as soon as she could and had just returned to his lodgings when Mrs Kelly had handed him the crumpled envelope.

"This came for you today." She had smiled, showing black gaps in between brown teeth. "From your lassie in Ireland, no doubt." Billy had held the envelope up to the gas mantle, hissing above the painted wooden mantelpiece, to see it clearer.

"No doubt, Mrs. Kelly," he had said. "No doubt."

He had broken the seal and read the childlike words and, as he did so, a chill touched his heart. Mary, with his child inside her. He had just managed to overcome his reluctance to marry at all as his feelings for Annie had deepened, and to be met with this ultimatum from Mary was more than he'd bargained for.

His first reaction was to get drunker than he had ever done in his life. But reason told him he had only himself to blame. And blame himself he did. There was only one way to sort things and that was to send for Mary and marry her and give the child his name. There would be plenty time for drinking after the wedding. And for telling Annie!

He had penned his answer to Mary that night, making sure to enclose enough money for her travel from Belfast to Dundee, and thought of Annie. How he wished with all his heart that it was she and not Mary who would be coming to be his wife, but wishing and longing only made his heart heavier. His next letter to Annie, was short and unemotional, written as it was on the day after his marriage and with the pain of the hopelessness he felt. If it was God's will he could not have her, then Mary would have to do. No child of his would bear the stigma of being a bastard.

The cold November wind had come in off the North Sea and swept through the iron structure of the railway station where Billy had waited, since late afternoon, for the train carrying Mary to arrive. The smell of jute which pervaded the town was, for once, diminished by the acrid mix of oil and smoke as it hissed and gushed from the steam-driven trains. The hands of the great station clock moved another minute nearer to six o'clock and Billy shifted uneasily in his polished boots. Memories of that night with Mary forced their way into his consciousness and mixed with thoughts of Annie by the river, Annie gathering the flax and Annie lying in his arms the night before he had left Ireland.

All at once, the train was there, in front of him, its wooden doors with their brass handles opening onto the station platform, the great hiss of steam and clouds of smoke filling his ears and his nostrils. People began to emerge from the carriages. His eyes had scanned the faces of men with bundles and women with wicker baskets, children pulling at their mother's skirts and porters scurrying to unload parcels and boxes. And then he had seen her. Somehow smaller than he had remembered and thinner, despite her condition. She carried a small carpet bag and a brown paper parcel tied with string. Her hair, which he recalled had been long and black, was hanging in waves either side of her pale face and her woollen shawl was pinned tightly across her breasts. She had looked for all the world like a startled rabbit lost in some strange place. Billy strode towards her.

"Mary!" he had said loudly over the noise of the station. "You're here." Their eyes met, hers scared and questioning and his concerned and unsure. "It's not far to walk… here, let me take your things, the journey must have exhausted you." Billy had heard his voice ramble on in its uncertainty. Despite his worldliness, he felt like a boy again, waiting for chastisement from his father.

He took her hand in his and together they walked in silence from the station along the length of Dock Street, before turning into Peep-o-Day lane which climbed up to meet the Blackscroft then up St Rouques Lane past Baxters Lower Dens Works and into King Street. Billy had pointed out the mill where he was overseer, running the length of Prince's Street, till it curved away around Crescent Street.

Mary had been struck by the size of the mills and the smell of the jute which seemed to fill her nostrils and drew closer to Billy. It was dark now and the street lamps were being lit by the Leeries with their long poles. The White Horse public house at the foot of Dens Brae spread an orange glow from its frosted glass windows as they passed and when the door had swung open, had revealed the smoke and brawl of the mill workers spending their hard earned shillings on whisky and beer.

They turned along Todburn Lane, cobbled and narrow with its closes leading into the back-lands of Dens Brae and the tenement homes of the mill workers, their children and their lodgers, sometimes living ten to a room. An old crone had hurried past, a clay pipe clamped between her teeth intent on filling her can with alcohol before the alehouse closed. She barely gave them a second glance.

"Nearly there," said Billy, his fingers numb around the string of Mary's parcel. He had led her up the winding stairwell she was to come to know so well and along the stone walkway to the brown door. "Here, hold these a minute." Mary took the bag and the bundle while Billy opened the door. She followed him into the darkness of a small lobby, which led into the kitchen. He had left the gas mantle turned low and red coal glowed in the range.

"Welcome home," he'd said simply, swinging the black kettle over the heat. "I suppose you wouldn't say no to some tea?"

Annie woke early, her hands still curled round her womb, her head immediately filling with the words of Billy's letter. She pulled herself free from the blanket and pushed her feet into her boots. The nuns were moving about, never seeming to need sleep and one of them approached Annie. She motioned her to follow, leading her down a long polished corridor to a chair. The nun disappeared through a door and returned moments later to usher Annie into a small room in which sat another nun, much older than the rest.

She smiled at Annie and made the sign of the cross.

"Please," she began. "Sit." Annie scraped the chair back over the wooden floor.

"I was sorry to hear of your mother's passing, Annie," the nun began. "But we've got to think on now, think of what we're going to do with yourself." Annie nodded.

"You know you can't stay here forever, don't you and what I need to know is… Do you have anywhere, Annie, you could go to?"

Annie lowered her head and stared at her hands, red and dry with the cold. She thought of Mary, married now to Billy and carrying his baby. "No," she answered, lifting her eyes to meet those of the Mother. "Nowhere… and…" She stared defiantly, fighting back the tears. "I'm with child."

The nun gazed at the young girl before her and shook her head. "Mother of God?, Annie, what have you done?" she sighed quietly.

Annie poured out the whole story, about Billy and Mary and Mrs Pepper and how she had always tried her best and may God forgive her. She never had been a fighter like Mary and the little courage she did have was overpowered by the fear she now felt, both for herself and her unborn child. Tears welled in her brown eyes and ran in salty rivers down her face.

The nun stood up. "Stop crying now, Annie," she instructed, sounding practical and calm. "I know you were a good daughter to your mother, and Father Dominic, who sent you and Mrs Pepper to us,spoke highly of your regular attendance at Mass. So I'm going to let you stay. You can work in the Laundry here to pay for your keep during your confinement, but once the baby is born Annie, you must give it up to be adopted. Do you understand? It's the only thing that can be done."

Annie was at once relieved and apprehensive. "But, Mother," she began.

"I don't know…"

The nun silenced her with a raised palm. "Go now and I'll pray to God that all will be well."

Annie returned to her bed in the dingy room she shared with the other women and pulled her box out from beneath it. She wrote to Mary, telling her of their mother's passing, but she couldn't bring herself to mention Billy, or the marriage, or the fact she also was carrying Billy's child. She had four months left of her confinement and was determined that when the baby was born, she would keep it; somehow, she would manage.

The following day, Annie awoke earlier than usual. It was still dark as she dressed and made her way to the laundry room, stopping only to drink some tea and eat a slab of soda bread. She had never ventured into the basement before and was unaware of the stark conditions in which she would spend twelve hours a day for the rest of her confinement, nor of the young girl with whom she would toil.

Coming in from the cold corridor which led to the Laundry intensified the wave of heat that hit Annie as she opened the heavy door. There were huge drums along the full length of one wall driven by steam pistons, solemnly turning and gurgling, there were metal closets full of racks on which layers of clothes were drying. Presses and mangles, sinks and tubs and water, hot, cold and tepid, was everywhere. Through the haze of steam and noise, Annie could see the shape of a girl and made towards it.

She tapped her on the shoulder, startling her in her soapy duty. The girl pushed the hair back from her red forehead and smiled nervously.

"Annie," Annie shouted over the noise of the steam pistons by way of introduction, and extended her hand. The girl ran her own hands down her apron to remove some of the suds and accepted the handshake.

"I'm to work here for the next while," Annie explained. "What do I do?" At that moment, one of the nuns emerged from the mist and came towards them. She motioned Annie towards a huge sink and a basket of what looked like thick woollen vests and wool stockings. Annie nodded and began the task of soaping and rinsing, squeezing and rubbing at the sweat-stained clothing till it was spotless. She forced their thickness through the iron mangle and hung them on one of the huge drying racks to finish off. Already her back was aching and her hands were scarlet and swollen with squeezing and rubbing the woollen cloth. She felt a movement at her shoulder. It was the young girl.

"It gets easier," she mouthed, smiling. "I'm Bella." She looked around for the nun and seeing no one, indicated to Annie to sit down beside her on a pile of unwashed bedding.

She could have been no more than sixteen, dark of eyes and hair and almost gypsy-like in her looks. She blushed under Annie's gaze, as if ashamed of being there.

Annie grinned at her. "I'm going to have a baby," she told Bella. "So I'll be here for a while… till it's time."

The girl's eyes opened in amazement and looked at Annie. "A baby!" she exclaimed. "When it comes, can I help you look after it?" she begged. "Love it and look after it?"

Annie was surprised at the request but smiled and nodded. "Of course you can. But first, there's all these sheets to wash. Best get on."

They returned to their respective toil but in that moment they had formed a bond which was to see Annie through the hardship and pain of the weeks and months to come.

From that day, Bella was by her side, working in the dreadful heat and damp, sharing the meagre food they got, so that Annie had the bigger share, for the baby's sake.

It was during her eighth month of pregnancy that the contractions started. At first, she had put it down to the usual aches and pains she lived with, lifting the sodden sheets and unloading the washing drums. She signalled to Bella to come over. A concerned Bella came at once.

"What is it, Annie?" she enquired, her young face flushed with the heat. Before she could answer, Annie felt a rush of wetness flow down her legs and a circle of pain clamp around her womb, holding her in a vice-like grip. She fell on her knees, unable to stand, amongst the pile of clothing waiting to be sorted.

"Bella," she screamed. "Get Sister Magdalen quickly."

Within minutes, Bella returned with the nun hurrying behind her.

"Can you move?" the nun asked Annie. Annie shook her head. "Then you'll have to have it here." She ordered Bella to get clean sheets and towels from the storeroom and tried to move Annie onto them, but the pain wouldn't allow. Annie had never known such agony and her screams could be heard above the noise of the presses and churning drums. Bella tried to comfort her and hold her head, but for two solid hours, the pain gripped Annie relentlessly. Her frame vibrated with each increasing wave of labour and just when she felt she could bear it no longer, the driving force of the child's head being expelled from its warm dark place inside Annie catapulted Billy's baby into the world.

She heard the nun mutter to Bella. "Fetch Sister Ignatius, Bella, as quickly as you can. The baby must be taken away from Annie immediately."

Annie struggled to raise herself up, her eyes wide with horror. "No," she wailed. "Don't take my child, please…" Bella froze.

Sister Magdalen wrapped the child in a white towel and held it to her. "I must take it, Annie, you know I must. He's to be adopted."

Annie jerked herself upright. "He," she repeated. "It's a son?" The nun nodded. "Please, please let me see his face," she begged. "Please."

The nun hesitated before answering Annie's plea. "Just once," said the nun. "Then he must go for adoption."

Annie gently pulled aside the towel and looked at her child. Billy's face, red and bloody, eyes tight shut and mouth gulping in its first breaths, lay before her. She looked at the nun, her eyes asking for some sign of relenting, but there was none. After quickly covering the baby's face, Sister Magdalen was gone. Bella sat motionless as Annie wept. "I'll look out for him Annie, I promise I'll find him for you and bring him back." But her childlike words fell on deaf ears as Annie fell into a depth of sorrow known only to those who grieve.

For ten days a black depression enveloped Annie. She cared not whether it was day or night or which way the wind blew, she felt only loss. Bella stayed with her as often as she could and tried to coax her to eat.

"Please, Annie," she begged. "Just a mouthful of soup to keep your strength up."

Annie obliged, but tasted nothing. She felt as if she were in the eye of a hurricane. All around her, things were moving; birds still sang in the early morning, food was cooked, wretched women came and went throughout the days into the room where she sat, void of feeling and perfectly still.

She asked God the same question, over and over. "Why are you punishing me?"

Every hour of every day that passed, she asked, but no answer came and, finally, she stopped asking.

But gradually, she became aware again. Nature began to heal her mind and body, despite the unwillingness of Annie's heart to cooperate.

The first thing to penetrate her stillness was Bella's voice, talking to her of everyday things. Her laundry work, the Sisters, the weather. Never seeking an answer, just talking in her soft, Irish voice. Slowly, Annie's appetite returned and eventually, much to the relief and delight of Bella, she was strong enough to begin again to work with her in the laundry.

The Spring arrived late that year and it aroused in Annie the need to be in the fresh air again. She had suffered much since her father's death and longed to be free of the past and even dared to hope for some happiness in the future. She was lost in her thoughts when she heard her name being called.

"Annie, Annie." Bella ran up to her breathless and grinning from ear to ear. "I've a letter for you." She held it up before her. "Sister Magdalen said to give it to you right away."

Annie took the small envelope in her hands and gazed at the childlike printing. The late Spring sunshine broke through the clouds as she opened it.

'Annie,' it began. 'I have to tell you my baby girl is born. She's called Nancy. Please come. I cried for Mammy. Here's money.' It was signed in Mary's childlike script.

Annie looked at the strange Scottish pound notes in her hand. "Is it good news?" Bella asked anxiously, fearful that Annie would go back into the blackness.

Annie nodded. "My sister wants me to come to Scotland, Bella. She's even sent the money for the fare."

Bella stepped back. "And will you go, Annie?" she asked, quietly, fearful of the answer.

Annie sighed in resignation. "What is there for me here, Bella? Mammy's dead and they've taken my son away from me." Annie folded the letter and returned it to its envelope along with the money. It was only then that she realised Bella's unhappiness. She put a comforting arm around her friend. "I only wish I could take you with me Bella, but I can't."

Bella nodded.

"Will you let me know where you are Annie, and if you're well?" she asked shakily.

Annie pulled her closer. "Of course I will… and I'll never forget your kindness, Bella, not as long as I live."

Taking her hand, Annie led Bella to the dormitory. She pulled the box out from under her bed and took out the linen handkerchief which held her father's watch and the silver brooch he had given her on her twenty-first birthday.

She pressed it into Bella's hand. "I'd like you to have this Bella. To remember me by, and to thank you for everything."

Bella gazed at the shining sliver gift. She had never seen anything so beautiful. "For me?" she asked Annie.

"For you."

The following week, Annie left the Poor House forever, carrying with her, her small bundle of possessions and a heart full of hope. She was going to Dundee and to the future.

CHAPTER 5

Mary's birth had been easy. A natural mother the midwife had called her. Nancy was the most beautiful child born, according to her father, and the birth seemed to have brought Billy and Mary closer than she had thought possible only a few months before.

The wedding had been quiet and, out of necessity, quick, as Billy had been determined the child would not be born out of wedlock. They had married in the vestibule of the Wishart Church in King Street, with Mary having to renounce her Catholic faith in favour of Billy's Protestant one. But she told herself it would be alright with God who, she was sure, would rather see her married to a Protestant, than giving birth to a bastard Catholic.

Mary was well aware that Billy's feelings for her were not as strong as they had been for Annie. He'd never told her he loved her, but had made sure she was well looked after. As an overseer at the mill, he earned over twenty-one shillings a week and, apart from the night of the wedding, when he had gotten blind drunk, hadn't spent a penny of it on whiskey or beer.

In her new status as his wife and Nancy's mother, Mary had felt happy and contented but when the letter had arrived from Annie, telling of their Mammy's passing in the Poor House, she had been overcome with guilt. She had left Annie and her mother to cope on their own when she left for Belfast and now deeply regretted her inadequacy. Of course, she had been pregnant, but no one had known that and it must have seemed like she was deserting them both.

She had approached Billy as soon as he had returned home from the mill that evening, showing him the letter from Annie.

"Can she come and live with us, Billy, please…" she had pleaded. "I've let her and Mammy down so badly and I can't bear the thought of her alone in the Poor House when we have so much… please, Billy, say she can come."

Billy placed the letter on the kitchen table and walked over to the wooden cradle where Nancy lay sleeping. He picked her up, careful not to waken her, and rocked her gently in his arms as he fought to control the surge of bittersweet emotion which rushed through him at the mention of Annie's name.

Mary waited.

"You know she's a hard worker, Billy. She'll soon find work to pay for her keep and she can share the back room with Nancy, once she's weaned."

Billy continued to rock his child.

"Billy," Mary pleaded again. "Please say she can come."

Without saying a word for fear his voice would betray his inner turmoil, Billy returned the sleeping Nancy to her cradle and went to the sideboard. He took out a small tea caddie where he kept the money he saved every week from his wages and counted out three pound notes.

Handing them to Mary, he nodded silently.

Mary threw her arms around him and kissed his cheek and neck. "You won't regret it Billy, I promise you won't." assured Mary.

"I know," said Billy, slowly removing her arms from his neck. "I know. Now then, Mary Dawson," he demanded in mock-firmness. "Where's my tea?"

The crossing on the boat from Belfast was uneventful for most people on board, but for Annie, it was the beginning of a new chapter in her life. She breathed in the salt air as she leaned over the ship's rail watching the waves rushing by as the sky shimmered blue and white over the sparkling water of the Irish Sea. The wind and sunshine on that day, succeeded in bringing the colour back to her cheeks and energy back to her body. Her very spirit seemed to rejoice in being alive and a new hope welled inside her.

She tried to imagine what Dundee would be like as her mind drifted along with the scurrying clouds. She was determined she would find work and somewhere to live as soon as she could, the thought of sharing the same house with Mary and Billy wasn't a prospect she was relishing but, in the short term, she reasoned, it was something she could cope with. Annie had missed Mary, with her quick tongue and zest for life. It had been a long time since they'd shared sisterly things together, but her feelings about seeing her again, especially with her baby, were decidedly mixed.

Not wanting anything to mar the brightness of her mood, Annie pushed the quiver of unease back down inside her. She was going to a new country, she told herself firmly, and a new life. Never again did she want to have to suffer the pain and grief which had so recently visited her. This was her chance, thanks to Mary, to live again and she would do nothing to spoil either her own life or her sister's, no matter what happened in the future.

Along with what seemed like the entire population of Scotland, Annie boarded the steam train at Glasgow which would take her on the last leg of her journey to Dundee. She unwrapped the meat pie she had purchased from a street seller outside the station and consumed it with relish. She had hardly eaten anything that day due to the excitement she had felt keeping her appetite at bay and couldn't remember enjoying anything to eat so much, except perhaps her mother's hot apple dumplings.

The train would its way through the gray grimness of the outskirts of Glasgow, through Lanarkshire and into Stirlingshire. Annie, her nose pressed to the glass of the window, watched with fascination as the landscape changed into the rolling countryside of Perthshire and the Strathmore Valley. In its wake, the train left a trail of white smoke and steam as it rattled along the rails. Annie looked at the other travellers sharing her carriage and tried to make sense of their Scottish accents.

Towards the end of the journey, one of her fellow travellers asked her if she was going all the way to Dundee. Apart from the word Dundee, she couldn't understand the rest, but nodded anyway.

"Well, we're nearly there, lassie."

The train began to slow, its huge wheels sparking and grinding as the engine driver applied the brakes. Annie read the word INVERGOWRIE as it pulled into the little station. The man across from her lowered the carriage window, holding the leather strap to slow its descent and thrust his head through the gap.

"We'll see the Tay Bridge soon, Chrissie, then we'll know we're home." His wife, Chrissie, rummaged in the bottom of the cloth bag on her lap and produced a hankie and proceeded to dab her forehead. The train gushed steam and began to move again and the iron girders of the Tay Bridge came into view. Annie craned her neck to see forward past the man, who looked as though he would fall out of the carriage onto the rails at any minute.

The bridge curved majestically from Dundee to the Fife shore as it spanned the tidal river and, as the train rounded the end of the bridge, Annie could see a wide road with trees overlooking the river.

"Is this Dundee?" she asked the man, shouting above the noise of the engine coming in through the carriage window.

"It is, lassie, Bonnie Dundee." The pride in his voice was obvious. "Aye, "he repeated. "Bonnie," and turning to Annie added, "Just like yourself."

Annie blushed with pleasure, all of a sudden feeling like a little girl again. The genuineness of the compliment made her feel warm inside as well as out. She was going to like Dundee, she decided, and its people.

The train slowed again and inched its way into Dundee's West Station. There was a scramble of activity as boxes and cases were lifted down from the racks above the seats.

"We're here," said the man, opening the carriage door and motioning to his wife to alight. Annie felt a little well of panic forming in her stomach. She hadn't told Mary when she would be arriving, or even if she would be arriving, and now she was here, she realised she didn't know how to get to Mary's house.

She tapped the man on the shoulder. "Please can you help me?" she asked.

"If I can, lassie," he replied.

"I need to get to William Lane… it's beside a jute mill," Annie ventured. The man laughed. "God, lassie, there's a mill on every street corner in this town, but I know well where William Lane is. We live in the Cowgate ourselves … follow us, and you'll not go wrong."

Although Annie barely understood his broad dialect, she nodded and moved after them through the vast railway station and out into the bustling, cobbled streets of Dundee.

The man and his wife were kindness itself, as they guided her along the wide road by the docks. She craned her neck to take in a huge stone archway through which horse-drawn carts were trundling, laden with cargo from the boats tied up at the quay.

"That's the Royal Arch," the man pointed out with pride. "Isn't she bonnie?"

Annie nodded and hurried after them. "Is it far to go?" she asked as she tripped over the uneven cobbles, more with tiredness than clumsiness. She was beginning to feel the weariness of the train journey seep into her bones.

"Past the Pillars, up through the Murraygate and into King Street," he replied. "That's where me an' Mrs Wilson will part company wi' yourself. But William Lane's just off King Street. Don't worry, you'll not get lost."

At the branch where Cowgate joined King Street, Annie waved the Wilsons goodbye and, muttering the directions to herself, she walked the last mile to Mary and Billy's home.

William Lane was narrow and steep, sloping upwards from King Street to join Victoria Road. A dark close ran off to the left, above which were two small windows covered inside with heavy curtaining. To the right was Todburn Lane, flanked by tall tenements and peppered with clumps of grass growing between the stone cassies. Two women were standing, arms folded over woollen shawls, watching a gaggle of street urchins playing Hopscotch.

They casually looked her way as Annie crossed over.

Now she was so near, Annie began to feel apprehensive again but there was to be no going back and with a deep breath, she turned into the entrance leading to Mary and Billy's tenement home.

A young woman, her hair hanging limply round her face and dressed in a rough black skirt and green knitted shawl, came running down the stairwell, almost bumping into Annie, who was trying to avoid a cat which lay asleep on one of the steps.

"Watch yourself," called the girl, steadying Annie with her hand.

"My fault, I'm sure," said Annie. She held on to the girl's arm. "Maybe you could help me anyway," Annie continued. "I'm looking for Mary Dawson, do you know her?"

The girl nodded. "The Dawsons live up there." She pointed. "Two stairs up second door from the end." Annie thanked her and made to climb the stair.

"But here's Mr Dawson anyway," she heard the girl call to her from the end of the close. "He'll take you up."

Despite her resolve and determination, Annie felt a wave of emotion surge through her at the words. This wasn't how she had wanted things to happen. Slowly she turned to face him.

"Annie?" he asked hesitantly. "Is it you?" Billy moved towards her. "It *is* you." For a moment Annie's whole world seemed to melt away as their eyes met.

"Why didn't you let us know you were coming?" He took her bundle, which she had carried all the way from Belfast, and hooked her arm under his.

"Mary'll be so pleased to see you again." The words kept coming towards her. "I was so sorry to hear about Mrs Pepper," he continued, leading her up another flight of stairs. "You must be desperate for some tea." They turned along the stone walkway.

"Mary!" Billy called out, knocking on the kitchen window as they passed it. "Guess who's turned up?"

Mary's head popped round the kitchen door. "Annie," she cried in delight. "You've come, you've come." She bustled her into the small kitchen. "You should've let us know Annie Pepper, Billy would have met you from the train."

Suddenly, Annie felt like the younger of the two sisters instead of the elder. Mary had changed so much. No longer the willful scatterbrain but a full-grown woman.

Her mother had always said that Mary needed a man to keep her in check and it looked like she'd been right. It was a pity, thought Annie, that the man had turned out to be Billy.

The turmoil in Annie subsided. She didn't know what she had expected, but was glad that Billy had been polite and kind, but no more than that expected of a brother-in-law and that Mary had welcomed her with such warmth. Neither Billy nor Mary knew about her own recent pregnancy and childbirth and Annie would make certain they never would. It was going to be alright, she told herself. Her only hurdle now was seeing her new niece, Nancy.

The tiny form of Nancy lay sleeping in her cradle as Mary and Annie tiptoed into the room.

Annie leaned over the infant.

"She's beautiful Mary," she whispered. "And she's the spittin' image of her Mammy." Annie was glad Nancy hadn't taken Billy's looks, as her own child had. That would have been too much for her to bear.

"Once she's weaned," continued Mary, "You'll have to share this room with her, if that's alright. But, till then," Mary shrugged her small shoulders. "This is yours alone."

The room was bigger than the kitchen, where most of the daily activity took place, including where Billy and Mary slept in their double bed in an alcove. The window faced South and in the late afternoon, the room still held the warmth of the earlier sun. A coal fire was on one wall, made ready for lighting and a heavy mahogany chest-of-drawers and a single bed sat along the other. In the corner near the window was a cot, ready for use when Nancy was weaned.

Two gas mantles were set either side of the mantelpiece and a wooden rocking chair and small table had been placed near the fire. The floorboards were covered in places by rag rugs and the curtains at the window were dark and heavy woven.

"I'll make us some tea," Mary announced, moving towards the door and leaving Annie alone in the room. She sat on the edge of the bed and undid her bundle. What little she had, she put into an empty drawer, including her father's watch. She thought of Bella and wondered how she was, back at that awful place Annie had so recently left. She must write to her, let her know where she was and maybe, one day, she would be able to see her again.

"Tea's ready," called Mary from the other room. Annie went through. The kitchen was darker than Annie's room and a fire burned in the range. At the window was a small sink with a cold water tap and a wooden draining board with a cupboard beneath. Mary indicated the table where she had placed two china cups and saucers and a pot of tea. Annie picked up her cup.

"Why Mary, they're the most delicate things I've seen, where did you get them?"

Mary smiled. "They're Billy's wedding present to me. There's only the two of them, but as this is such a special occasion, I thought I'd bring them out. They're normally wrapped in paper in the bottom of the sideboard." She laughed. "Seem to have got into mammy's habit of saving things for 'good', even though Billy's earning enough money that I could probably afford a full set if I wanted one." She poured the brown liquid into the cups.

"Will you be alright, Annie?" she asked quietly. "I know how it was for you, fancying Billy and all, but things are different now, especially since the baby…"

"I'm fine" interrupted Annie, not wanting the conversation to go any further. "All I want is to find work and a place for myself, Mary. I won't be any trouble at all, in fact, you and Billy won't even know I'm here."

She hoped her voice had not betrayed her feelings for Billy which, she now knew, were still very much alive, but Mary seemed re-assured.

"We'll talk no more about it then," she said. "Tomorrow Billy's going to ask about work for you at the mill and Nancy and me will take you to the Greenmarket. Oh, Annie, it'll be like old times again."

Annie's eyes misted over at the sight of her sister's happiness. "That'll be just the ticket Mary, and can I push the pram?"

Both women laughed together and drank their tea. It was good to be part of a family again and Annie silently reaffirmed her vow that she would do nothing to upset Mary, no matter what.

Billy was as good as his word and came home with the news that Mr Campbell, the mill manager wanted to see Annie at his office at nine o'clock the next day to 'look her over.' Billy had told him she was his sister-in-law and a hard worker, but Mr Campbell wanted to see her for himself before deciding to offer her work.

"What sort of work could I do in the mill?" she asked Billy, suddenly worried that she might let everyone down, including herself.

"There's lots of jobs in the mill, Annie, mostly done by women an' all. This town's not like anything you've ever known, it's the women who work in Dundee, while the men turn a shilling where they can. It's cheaper for the mill owners that way and, anyway, the women's fingers are nimbler. Don't worry, Annie, you'll be fine," he reassured her. "You know about the flax don't you? Hasn't your daddy grown enough of it in his time and we've harvested it too…" Billy's voice stopped in mid-sentence and he abruptly stood up and crossed to the sink, turned on the cold tap and vigorously began washing his hands. "Nine o'clock tomorrow," he called over his shoulder. "Mr Campbell's expecting you."

"Right," said Annie, shakily. "Nine o'clock it is." A small frown of worry formed on Mary's brow.

At precisely 8.45, Annie presented herself at the Mill in her best and only jacket, hoping Mr Campbell wouldn't notice the scruffiness of her boots which, despite vigorous polishing the night before, refused to take on a shine.

"You've to see Mister Cambell, you say?" quizzed the gatekeeper, emerging from behind the small window that overlooked the entrance to the mill, looking Annie up and down. "A job is it?"

Annie nodded.

"This way."

Annie followed the gatekeeper across the cobbled yard, through a door and up a steep flight of wooden stairs to an office marked, 'Manager' and beneath the title, the name, 'A Campbell'. He knocked at the door.

"Come," said a deep voice.

The gatekeeper opened the door and leaned in. "It's a woman about a job," he whispered almost reverently. "Says she's to see you at nine. Will I show 'er in?"

There was a momentarily silence before the gatekeeper re-emerged and bustled Annie through the door, closing it quietly behind her.

"Sit," Mr Campbell instructed, continuing to write at the huge walnut desk. "Annie Pepper, is it?"

Annie nodded.

"Speak up young woman," he snapped, not hearing any reply.

"Yes," Annie answered quickly. "I'm here looking for work."

Mr Campbell returned his pen to its holder and replaced the lid of the ink bottle, before looking at her for the first time. "And what kind of work can you do?" he enquired.

Annie gulped. Mr Campbell was a big man with gray hair and a bushy moustache completely covering his upper lip. Annie wondered how he managed to eat.

"Well?" Mr Campbell continued.

Annie's wits seemed to have deserted her. "Anything at all," she managed to mutter.

"What do you mean, anything? Can you spin, weave, wind, sweep the floors?"

Annie felt panic overwhelming her. "Yes," she agreed anxiously. "I can sweep floors."

Mr Campbell sat back in his chair and looked at her. "Let's see your hands," he commanded. Annie stretched out her hands in front of her. "Mmmmhhh, long fingers, that's good," he muttered to himself. "Billy Dawson says you're a hard worker, Annie Pepper. Is that right?"

"Yes, Mr Campbell, I'm a very hard worker," Annie replied.

"Are you a fast learner too, Annie Pepper?"

Annie nodded. Mr Campbell leaned back further in his chair and swivelled it around to face her straight on.

"Report to Mr Dawson tomorrow at seven o'clock. Tell him I said you've to learn the weaving. You'll start on seven shillings and sixpence a week till you can handle a pair of frames, then it'll go up to twelve shillings and sixpence." He returned to his paperwork and dismissed Annie with a flick of his hand. "And don't be late," he added. "Timeliness and Godliness is what Baxters expects from you, nothing less."

Annie backed out of Mr Campbell's Office and skipped down the wooden stairs. "I start tomorrow," she called to the gatekeeper, beaming all over her face.

The gatekeeper returned her smile. "We'll see you tomorrow then. Welcome to Baxters."

Early next morning, Annie joined the throng of cloth-capped men and apron-clad women as they streamed through the mill gates. The air was full of chatter and calling to one another and Annie noticed a few nudges and glances from a group of women as she passed through the gate and into the yard. One of them broke away from the others and came towards her.

"You're new!" she stated, smiling at Annie.

"Yes, it's my first day."

"Irish too!" she continued, noticing her accent. "Weavin' or spinnin'?"

"Weaving I think. I've to see Mr Dawson."

"I'm a Weaver myself', it'll probably be me who shows you what to do."

The two women moved through into a huge area filled with machinery slung with leather belts and iron wheels. Large spools holding yarn sat at each machine and women were already busy pulling the long threads through rows of holes in a metal bar at the front of the machine and tying them off, while young boys stacked loaded bobbins beside empty shuttles.

"They're gettin' the looms ready for the weavers," she advised Annie. "That's my pair over there." She pointed in the direction they were heading. Annie hurried after her down the long passageway to the end of the weaving flat.

"There's Mister Dawson over there. C'mon, I'll take you over." She guided Annie to the white-coated figure of Billy.

"She's the new start, Mister Dawson. 'Do you want me to show 'er the ropes?"

Billy turned and smiled at Annie. "Are you alright?" he enquired. Annie nodded.

"Right, Jessie. Get her shifting for you this week and tying on and let her see how a weaver earns her crust." Jessie grinned and indicated to Annie to follow her.

"I'll no' be able to speak to you when the looms start up, so just watch everything I do."

Almost before she'd finished speaking the great looms leaped into life. Annie couldn't believe the noise that filled her ears, followed by the dust that began to fly from the vibrating yarn, filling her nose and throat. She looked at Jessie and indicated her ears.

Jessie laughed and shook her head. This was something Annie would have to get used to if she was to become a weaver. By midday, Annie was beginning to adjust to the noise but was relieved when the wailing of a siren indicated to the workers it was time to eat. The Weavers switched off their machines and, although silence returned to the weaving flat, Annie's ears were ringing.

"You heard the 'bummer' then?" Jessie enquired. "Break time again. Have you brought something to eat or are you going home?" Jessie enquired.

Annie produced two chunks of bread sandwiched together with a little jam from her apron pocket. "My sister gave me this before I left this morning. Can we sit somewhere to eat?"

Annie followed Jessie to the door of the mill and out into the sunshine. Some of the men were kicking a ball around the yard, but most were eating or just chatting. A few nodded to them as they went past, and Jessie headed for her place by the wall in the shade where some of the other women were already eating their meagre fare.

Most of the chatter, Annie couldn't quite grasp, but she tried to answer any question directly aimed at her. "Mister Dawson, your brother-in-law is he?"

"Yes," replied Annie. "He's married to my sister, Mary."

"Was it him that got you in, then?"

"If you mean, is she here 'cause she knows the Gaffer, then you'd be right," interrupted Jessie. "An' she's a good wee worker, so mind your tongue."

The other woman fell silent as the 'bummer' signalled the end of the break.

"C'mon, Annie, time we got back to work."

Annie followed Jessie back to the weaving flat. "Watch that one," warned Jessie. "She's got a shine for Mister Dawson. She'd do anything to get her hands on 'im."

The looms screamed into life again and Annie bent to her task. Fetching the bobbins and helping Jessie when the threads broke and the looms had to be reset.

"Get the Tenter," shouted Jessie, agitated, when the yarn broke for the umpteenth time that afternoon. "Fetch Joe Cassiday."

Annie ran to the end of the flat where two men were working on a loom.

"I'm lookin' for the Tenter, Joe Cassiday, have you seen him?"

One of the men turned. "I'm Cassiday," he shouted. "What's the trouble?"

Annie couldn't believe she understood him, till she realised, he too, was Irish.

"Jessie's loom needs looking at."

Joe Cassiday nodded. "I'll be with you in a jiffy," he smiled. "Tell her Joe's on the job."

Annie nodded and made her way back down the walkway to Jessie's loom, looking back only once, but looking back just the same.

"He's on the way," she signalled to Jessie.

Joe Cassiday was as Irish as his name, with black hair, blue eyes and a smile that was as broad and generous as his nature. As he strolled down the passage towards them, Annie noticed that every woman in the flat was watching him go by. He'd wave to the ones who caught his eye and they all made sure they waved back.

Jessie nudged Annie in the ribs and nodded towards the approaching Tenter. "Makes me wish I was single again, Annie. Is he no' the best-lookin' man you've seen round here?"

Annie giggled at Jessie's expression as she gazed in admiration at Joe.

"Now, Jessie Greig," Joe demanded, leaning languidly on the machinery but pretending impatience. "Sure you're the worst Weaver in the whole of Baxters, so you are, always breaking something, including my heart."

Jessie beamed with pleasure. "Less o' that, Joseph Cassiday," she chided. "Remember I'm a married woman." They both roared with laughter as Joe set about fixing the loom.

Annie watched his skilled hands, tightening the belts and cleaning and greasing the nuts and shafts where they attached to the weaving frame. He threw a switch and the loom sprung back to life.

"There you are, Jessie, all better now. And don't you go breaking it again."

Jessie waved him off and Annie, like all the other women in the weaving flat, watched him go.

CHAPTER 6

The hours were long and the work hard, but Annie was happy. She learned quickly and was soon asking Jessie how long it would be before she could be trusted with looms of her own.

"Not long now, Annie," Jessie assured her. "I'll have a word wi' Mister Dawson this Saturday." Annie beamed. She liked Jessie Greig with her optimism and acceptance of a life, which had not been kind to her. She had given birth to six children, four daughters and two sons. The sons were ten and eleven years now and were themselves 'half-timers' in the neighbouring Lower Dens Mill, working for half of the day and attending the Wallacetown School for the rest. All of Jessie's daughters had died in infancy, two from Meningitis, one from Tuberculosis and one from Diphtheria. Her husband, Eddie, was always out of work and spent his time drinking in the Thrums Bar or picking up any casual labour he could get, either at the docks or in one of the jute warehouses.

At home, things were settling into a routine and with both Annie and Billy out working most of the time, Mary was left to deal with all the household chores, as well as looking after Nancy. Sunday was the only day they were all together, and it was then that Annie would volunteer to take Nancy out for long walks in her pram. This served a double purpose. It got Annie out into the fresh air, after her week in the mill and also away from the cosy domesticity Mary shared with Billy.

It was on one of these walks, through the town and out the Nethergate to Magdalen Green that Annie had her second encounter with Joe Cassiday. She was sitting on a bench overlooking the River Tay and watching the trains puffing over the railway bridge to Fife or winding their way along the waterside on their journey to Perth. It wasn't so long ago when Annie herself was on one of these trains coming into Dundee and she breathed a deep sigh of contentment at how much better things were now. She'd written to Bella, as she'd promised, telling her about her new job at the mill, and Mary and the baby.

She had often wished that Bella could share her good luck and was overjoyed when she had received a happy letter back from her. The nuns had found work for her as a scullery maid in the house of a doctor and his wife in Belfast. It was a fine house, with rooms upstairs and down and Bella had been given a small room in the attic of her very own. She worked in the kitchen and sometimes helped the Cook by peeling vegetables and chopping wood for the ovens. The Cook gave her extra food, because of her thinness and the Doctor and his wife were very kind to her.

They had a little baby son which Cook said was a gift from God and looked like an angel. She thanked Annie again for the brooch and said she wore it every Sunday to Mass.

It was in the midst of this reverie that Annie felt a tap on her shoulder. Startled, she turned to see the smiling face of Joe Cassiday.

"Well, well," he grinned. "Fancy meeting you here."

Annie, for some reason, blushed under his gaze. "I'm out walking the baby," she replied, pointing to the pram where Nancy's sleeping head peeped out from its woollen blanket.

Joe peered into the pram. "Yours?" he enquired.

"Oh, *no*!" Annie answered, a little too quickly. "It's me sister Mary's. She's called Nancy."

They both fixed their eyes on the sleeping babe as Joe sat down next to Annie on the bench.

"Sure, it's a fine day for walking babies," he announced.

"It is," Annie agreed.

"And is this fine city to your liking?"

"It is."

Annie's mind was racing with all manner of interesting things she could say to Joe but, her tongue seemed to have forgotten how to speak. Becoming more uncomfortable under Joe's gaze, she finally managed to blurt out, "And it's time I was getting back… Nancy will be wanting her tea soon."

The announcement of her imminent departure came as a shock to Joe, rather used to women being left behind by him.

"Perhaps you'll allow me to walk back with you?" he asked rapidly. "As long as you don't expect me to push that thing," he added, pointing to the pram. Annie giggled at Joe's pained expression and felt her vocal chords unfreeze.

"You'd probably have the baby tipped into the street at the first kerb," she countered, standing up and smoothing her best, and only, Sunday dress.

For once, Joe didn't have a reply and instead, took Annie's arm and guided her and the baby along the narrow path and back on to the pavement.

"It's a fine University they've got here," Joe commented, his eyes scanning the grey stone frontage of the seat of learning, across the road from the Green. "Wouldn't it be wonderful to have an education," he continued. "Not just learning your letters but really learning something, like engineering or doctoring."

"But you're a skilled man, Joe," Annie exclaimed in surprise. "Jessie says you're the best Tenter in Baxters."

Joe grinned again, his whole face lighting up. "*Only* in Baxters?" he repeated in mock astonishment. "And here's me thinking I was the best Tenter in the whole world."

The both laughed and turned to go back home.

"Do you stay near the mill?" Joe asked after they'd been walking for half an hour or so.

"William Lane," advised Annie.

Joe stopped in his tracks. "And don't I live in Todburn Lane, just round the corner from you."

They both congratulated themselves on how much they had 'in common'.

"So you live in William Lane, with your sister Mary and the baby…"

"And Mary's husband, Billy," Annie interrupted.

"Right," continued Joe. "And you're learning the weaving from Jessie. There's only one piece of the jigsaw missing!" exclaimed Joe.

"And what's that?" asked Annie.

Joe leaned against a lamp post and pushed back his bonnet. "Why, your name?"

"Annie Pepper," said the blushing young lady.

"Annie Pepper," Joe repeated. "What a fine name."

As they turned into William Lane, two of the women from the mill were gossiping at the end of their close.

"Fine day," commented Joe as they walked past, lifting his bonnet and inclining his dark head.

"For some, right enough," came the retort as they returned to their gossiping.

"I'll bet you any money, we're the talk of Baxters tomorrow," he whispered in Annie's ear. "I can see my reputation's going to be ruined… seen out with a strange woman pushing a pram."

"Get away with you, Joe Cassiday," Annie chided wickedly. "It's my reputation you should be worrying about. Imagine being seen out with the daftest man in Dundee."

"Daft am I?" Joe smiled, sparking his boots off the kerbstone. "Daft enough to be asking you to go out with me, Annie?"

Annie was taken aback at the suddenness of his words. "Go out with you?" she repeated trying to keep the tremor out of her voice. "And where would we go out to?" It was she who felt daft now, behaving like a sixteen year old who'd never been asked out before, which, apart from not being sixteen, was exactly true.

Joe looked at the pavement, considering his answer. "How about coming to Baxters Park with me next Sunday? We could take the tram."

An excitement welled inside Annie, and all thoughts of Billy suddenly dimmed. "Baxters Park it is, Joe," she replied sweetly, regaining some of her composure.

Joe grinned his biggest grin yet. "I'll wait for you here, at the end of the close on Sunday at one o'clock." He stepped backwards, almost falling off the kerb. Annie giggled like a schoolgirl. "And don't be late," he added mischievously, "I'm not a man who likes to be kept waiting."

Nancy began to wriggle in her pram and bawl for food.

"I won't Joe," she said softly, wheeling the pram into the close. "I won't."

Mary was preparing their dinner when Annie came into the kitchen with the squealing Nancy.

"Give her here Annie," instructed Mary, hugging the baby to her. "Did you have a nice walk then?" she cooed to Nancy.

"We had a delightful walk," replied Annie, smiling. "Quite delightful."

The lilt in Annie's voice made Mary look up.

"Next week," Annie continued coyly, "I'll be going to Baxters Park but, unfortunately, sister, I won't be able to take Nancy with me."

"You're going alone?" Mary queried.

"No," said Annie. "I'm going with Joe Cassiday." Annie couldn't keep the excitement out of her voice. "He's only asked me to go out with him Mary, and him the handsomest man in the whole of the mill."

She twirled around the room.

"Why, Annie Pepper!" Mary exclaimed. "What's been going on at that mill *and* under Billy's nose too?"

The mention of Billy's name made Annie stop twirling. 'Yes Mary,' she agreed secretively. 'Under Billy's nose too.'

"What's all this chattering then?" asked Billy, coming into the kitchen just in time to hear his name mentioned. "What's under my nose?"

Annie felt herself fluster. "It's something and nothing Billy," she murmured, removing her hat and coat and almost rushing out of the room. "I'll just put these things away."

Billy looked at Mary, bafflement in his eyes. "What on earth's got into her then?"

"She's a bit over-excited Billy, she's going to Baxters Park, I believe."

"And what's so exciting about Baxters Park?" asked Billy.

"Oh, it's not the park that's the exciting bit," continued Mary, now beginning to enjoy the intrigue. "It's who's taking her."

"And who is taking her?" asked Billy quietly, a stillness coming into his voice.

"Someone called Joe, Joe Cassiday." Mary began to feed Nancy and didn't see Billy's features change. "Cassiday, the Tenter?" he asked. "From the mill?"

"Well, I don't know if he's a Tenter, Billy," responded Mary, still tending to her baby. "But I'm sure he works at the mill." Mary looked up to see Billy's back disappearing out of the kitchen door and onto the landing outside. "Billy," she called. "Your dinner's nearly ready. Where are you off to?" But Billy had gone.

All that week, Annie anticipated her day out with Joe. Most of the time she was looking forward to it, but some of the time, she wasn't. Apart from Billy, she had never been in a man's company, not romantically anyway, whereas she was sure Joe had taken out lots of girls, if the obvious admiration of the other women was anything to go by.

Jessie noticed the change in her from the minute she arrived at the mill on Monday morning.

"You're needin' a good shake the day, Annie," she commented as they ate their midday food. "Are you feelin' alright? No' sickenin' for somethin' are you?"

"No, Jessie," she replied dreamily.

"I had a word with Mister Dawson on Saturday, about givin' you your own looms."

Annie paid attention. "And did he say I was ready, Jessie?"

"Well, he did on Saturday, but he seems to have changed his mind about it. I expected 'im over first thing to see me, but he's no' been near."

Annie couldn't hide her disappointment. She decided to speak to Billy herself.

"I've a message to go," she told Jessie, abruptly. "I'll see you later." Annie made her way back to the weaving flat where Billy was sitting at his desk writing up the yardage for the morning.

"Can I have a word, please, Billy?" she asked quietly.

Billy continued writing.

"Jessie says she spoke to you on Saturday, about me getting my own pair of looms…"

Billy continued to write.

"And I just want to know," she continued, "If I can?"

"You're not ready yet," Billy pronounced flatly, still not looking up.

"But, Billy," protested Annie. "if I was on a weaver's wage, I'd be able to rent a place of my own and…"

Billy stood up. "You're not ready yet," he repeated. "I'll tell you when." The coldness in his eyes took Annie by surprise.

"Right," she said, backing down. "Thanks." There were tears in her eyes as she ran back to Jessie's looms. This was a side of Billy she had never seen before and it hurt and frightened her.

Jessie returned to find Annie feverishly filling the shuttle boxes with trembling fingers. She put her hand on her arm and turned Annie round to face her.

"What's up Annie?" she asked, concern in her voice.

Annie's lips quivered. "He says I'm not ready, Jessie… I don't think he'll ever let me be a weaver."

Jessie relaxed. "God, lassie, I thought something was seriously wrong." She put her arm round Annie. "You'll make a fine weaver," she consoled her. "Just bide your time."

Annie smiled weakly and nodded. "Now, let's get on with the job in hand."

Billy had changed towards her, the kindness he had shown her as a brother-in-law, was suddenly gone, and in its place was a sternness verging on anger.

She tried even harder to avoid contact with him, both at the mill and at home.

Somehow, she decided, she must earn enough money to afford a place of her own, especially now that her feelings for Billy seemed to have dwindled. She found it hard to understand that this was the man she had loved with all her heart and now she could feel nothing but fear of him.

The morning of her trip to the park with Joe began under a cloudless sky, but by one o'clock the sun had gone. She brushed her auburn hair till it shone and tied it back with a blue ribbon to match her dress.

"You'll do, Annie Pepper," she told herself, taking a last look in the mirror above the mantelpiece. Mary and Billy were in the kitchen when she went through and Mary looked at her as she entered.

"Well, will you just look at you," Mary spoke admiringly. "I don't think I've ever seen you looking so pretty, Annie. Look Billy? Doesn't she look nice?" But Billy was already looking at her, his eyes a mixture of sadness and resignation.

"You look very nice, Annie," he said, almost to himself.

"Well," said Annie, beginning to feel uncomfortable under his gaze. "I'll be off then."

She walked past Billy's chair and felt his hand brush against her skirt as she went. There was a time when this action would have sent her spirits soaring but now, she felt only irritation. She closed the door and inhaled the outside air deeply. Joe was waiting.

"Isn't it a beautiful day for a walk in the park?" he announced more than asked. Annie looked quizzically at the gray sky as Joe held out his arm for her to link into. "We'll catch the quarter-past tram if we run," he told her, quickening both his and Annie's steps. "We don't want to waste any of this beautiful day."

The tram rumbled up Princes Street and along the Arbroath Road, stopping at the iron gates of Baxters Park. Joe lifted Annie from the tram onto the pavement. Again, the feeling of being sixteen swept over her.

"Put me down, Joe Cassiday," she scolded him, blushing pink. "Heaven knows who's looking at us."

"I don't care who's looking at us, Annie Pepper," he grinned. "I've been looking forward to this day all week and nothing's going to spoil it. C'mon."

The grass all around them was as green as the remembered grass of their homeland. Beds of flowers were splashed either side of their path and benches awaited tired strollers in the shelter of leafy shrubs. Ahead of them were the steps to a stone pavilion and promenade where couples were walking and before them lay the expanse of the park that seemed to have been put there especially for them that day.

Their feet, used to pavements and stone floors, walked silently on the soft grass, with only the whisper of Annie's dress betraying movement. Annie breathed deeply.

"This is lovely, Joe," she told him. "And it is a beautiful day." Joe pulled her arm tighter through his in agreement.

"Wait here," he instructed at the foot of the steps up to the pavilion. "And don't move."

He returned moments later with two large ice-cream cornets and handed one to Annie.

"I hope you like ice-cream," he smiled.

Annie licked the white swirl of coolness. "Mmmmhhh" she responded, closing her eyes and savouring the sweetness. It's the nicest ice-cream I've ever tasted, Joe."

"Let's sit for a while," he said, guiding Annie to a bench underneath the arches of the pavilion, where they finished their treat.

"How'd you like living with your sister and her man?" Joe asked leaning forward, his elbows on his knees and his eyes examining the backs of his hands.

Annie leaned forward too, sensing a seriousness that had crept into his voice. "It's fine," she replied. "Why do you ask?"

Joe leaned back. "I just wondered," he said, still not looking at her. "Knowing that Billy Dawson's your brother-in-law as well as your overseer."

It was Annie's turn to be serious now. "I'm not saying they've not been good to me, 'cause they have, specially Mary, but I'll be looking to find a place of me own as soon as Billy says I'm ready for the weaving."

Joe exhaled the breath he had been holding. "But, do you like living with them," he persisted. "Billy, I mean…"

Annie felt a twinge of unease form somewhere inside her. "Billy," Annie repeated, at once wondering why he was anxious to know and if it was possible, somehow, that Joe knew about her and Billy.

Joe turned and looked her full on. "Yes, Annie, Billy." His voice was now low and steady.

The twinge of unease developed into a knot.

"He's my sister's husband," she said. "That's all…"

The smile returned to Joe's face. "That's what I wanted to hear." He swallowed, taking her hand. "Race you to the gate."

The wind rushed over Annie's face, blowing away the seriousness of the last few minutes and by the time they had reached the gate, the grin was back on Joe's face.

"Tram or Shanks's Pony?" Joe enquired gallantly.

"If you mean do I want to walk home…" Annie looked at the sky as the first spots of rain began to fall and back at Joe. "I'd like nothing better."

Annie skipped up the winding stairs to Mary's front door. Her hair was wet, her dress was damp and her shoes squeaked but her eyes shone and her cheeks were rosy with colour. Joe had asked her out the following Sunday and his handshake, as he bade her goodbye, had lingered longer than it should have.

Mary was alone in the kitchen when Annie entered.

"Mary, "she called sweetly. "I've had the most wonderful day." She flopped into Billy's armchair, pushing the wet hair back from her forehead. "We walked in the park and Joe bought me ice-cream and we were on the tram, Mary," she sparkled. "It was the loveliest day of my entire life…" She had been so caught up in her own happiness, she had failed to see her sister's downcast eyes.

"Why, Mary!" exclaimed Annie, suddenly concerned. "What's wrong?"

"Nothing's wrong," answered Billy's voice behind her.

Annie swung round. Billy had come through from the other room. "Nancy's sleeping now," he informed Mary coldly. His eyes turned on Annie. "I think that's my chair," he stated. Annie jumped up, the colour in her cheeks disappearing under his stare.

"Sorry, Billy," she replied, glancing at Mary for some explanation. But Mary continued to avoid her eyes. "I'll just go through to my room," she muttered, moving towards the door.

"Arn't you going to tell me about your day out Annie?" Billy's voice cut through the atmosphere which had enveloped her. He unfolded a newspaper and held it up in front of him. "Did Joe show you a good time then?"

The emphasis on the words 'good time' hit Annie like a stone. Her heart racing, she returned to the kitchen. Billy continued to fix his eyes on the print and Mary to fix hers on the floor.

"Why do you ask, Billy?" she enquired, endeavouring to keep the strain out of her voice.

Billy looked up from his newspaper, anger etched on his forehead. "Because no sister-in-law of mine is going to bring disgrace on this house by associating herself with the likes of Joe Cassiday." Billy spat the words at her. He stood up and moved nearer her. "You'll *not* see him again and continue to live here," he stated, his voice cold.

Annie felt herself flush with a mixture of fear and panic. "Then let me be a weaver," she responded, the words rushing out of her. "And I'll get a place of me own."

Billy stood motionless. "I'll let you be a weaver, Annie Pepper," he told her, his stance hardening from cold to ice, "When you stop all this nonsense about Joe Cassiday, and not before." Annie held his eyes. Why was he wanting to spoil things for her, didn't he have Mary and the baby and a good job? Wasn't that enough for him?

Fearful of the consequences of answering, Annie turned away and walked from the small kitchen, with its sudden grimness, into her room, closing the door quietly behind her.

Nothing and no one would stop her seeing Joe, especially not Billy, she vowed.

Annie slept little that night, lying staring at the darkened ceiling and listening to Nancy's breathing as she slumbered soundly in her cot.

Thoughts rushed through her head for what seemed like hours. The Poor House, where she'd given birth to Billy's child and from where she'd buried her mother. The farm, her dead father. Eventually tears and tiredness began to cloud the memories. How she missed her father. He'd have sorted Billy out, she was sure of that. He would have sorted everything. Annie finally slept, only to be wakened again almost instantly, she felt, by the sound of the 'Knocker-Up' tapping the window.

She was both desperate and fearful to see Joe at the mill. Her every move, she was now sure, would be watched.

CHAPTER 7

The mill sprang into life as looms began their clacking. Jessie eyed Annie with concern. She had been worried about her ever since Billy had spoken to her and was now even more worried when she saw the despondency in her eyes. But there was no opportunity to speak to her over the noise of the mill and it was midday before she managed to sit Annie down in a quiet corner on a bundle of cloth.

"Are you going to tell me what's wrong, Annie?" she asked, her concern causing her to be more abrupt than she wanted to be.

Annie looked at her. "It's nothin' you can do anything about, Jessie," she replied sadly.

"Is it all this nonsense about Mister Dawson no' makin' you a weaver yet?"

Annie gazed into the middle distance and shook her head.

"Do you want me to see 'im for you?" she continued.

"No," Annie replied quickly, not wanting Jessie to risk her job and incur Billy's wrath.

"If it's no' the weavin' lassie, then what is it?"

Jessie's concern touched Annie's emotions and she felt her throat tighten. "Oh, Jessie," she began. "He says I've not to have anything to do with Joe and I've to never see him again."

Jessie looked perplexed. "Joe?" she queried. Annie nodded.

"Joe Cassiday?"

Jessie threw her head back and began laughing. "Would you stop frightening the wits out of me?" she gurgled. "Is that all that's wrong? Listen, take it from me, there's no use worryin' yourself about men, Annie. I've yet to meet one that's worth your tears."

The older woman shook her head. "If I'd had a daughter, I'd have wanted her to be just like you, Annie, so I'll speak to you like a mother. "You're tellin' me that Mister Dawson'll no' make you a weaver till you stop seein' Joe." Annie nodded. "Then stop seein' him, just for a wee while, till he does make you a weaver, then once you've got your looms, start seein 'im again!"

Annie's eyes clouded. "But that's deceitful Jessie," she whispered. "Lying and that."

"No more deceitful than what your brother-in-law's doing to you."

Annie smiled weakly. "Do you think it would work, Jessie?" she asked slowly.

Jessie patted her hand. "Take it from a wise woman, Annie, it'll work. Now, eat your dinner, it's nearly time to knock on again."

Annie decided to speak to Joe the following Sunday and explain things. She was sure he'd understand and once she could afford a place of her own, she would be free to see him as often as she wanted.

Although Annie felt better, now she could feel hopeful again, the atmosphere at home deteriorated as the week went on. No matter what Annie did to avoid Billy she always seemed to find herself in his company, when he would sit and watch her every move. Mary was becoming more and more reclusive and distant from both her and Billy, and Annie could sense that, before long, something was going to erupt.

On the Sunday she was to meet Joe again, Billy seemed to be watching her closer than ever. In an effort to keep the tension in check she offered to make him some tea.

Billy seemed pleased. "Now, that's more like it Annie," he said, taking the cup from her and brushing her hand with his as he did so.

"Where's Mary?" she asked quickly turning back to the range with the teapot.

"Salvation Army," answered Billy, morosely. "She's taken to going there a lot lately, seems she knows someone from the old country who's come over to the Army Hall at the foot of Wellington Street." Annie sipped her tea and looked at the clock.

Billy immediately noticed. "Goin' somewhere, Annie?" he asked coldly.

"Just for a walk," Annie replied quietly, looking down at her cup and hoping Billy would drop the subject. The sound of the ticking clock and Billy's breathing filled her with anxiety, until she felt her own breathing would stop.

She jumped up, almost spilling the remains of the tea in her cup. "Well," she quivered, trying to sound confident. "I'll just get my coat." Annie moved towards the other room but Billy caught her hand as she passed.

"If you think Joe Cassiday's waitin' for you," he hissed. "Think again." The menace in Billy's voice was tangible. Annie spun round and wrenched her arm free.

"Get away from me Billy," she breathed, real fear now washing over her. But Billy kept coming forward.

"You never used to say that to me Annie, remember?" He was towering over her now and Annie began to tremble. His hands held her again. "You know how I feel about you," he told her, his breathing becoming more laboured. "What's that Joe Cassiday got that I haven't, then, Annie? *Tell me*," he shouted at her. The tension that had been coursing through Billy exploded.

Annie's mind and heart were racing. "*Stop*, Billy," she cried, hysteria taking over, "*Please stop*." But Billy was no longer listening. He pushed her onto the double bed in the kitchen alcove and lay on top of her. The stubble on his face scraped over Annie's neck and cheeks as he forced his lips over hers. Sweat poured off him and Annie willed herself to faint as his hand pulled the top of her dress open.

The sound of Nancy crying in the other room filtered through Annie's distress. "*Billy*," she called out, attempting to push him away. "*Billy*, it's the baby crying, it's *Nancy*. Please, let me go to her." The noise of Billy's attack had woken the sleeping child and her cries seemed to bring Billy to his senses. He suddenly rolled his weight off her and covered his face with his hands.

"See to her," he muttered. Annie pushed herself up and ran through to her sister's child.

She picked up Nancy and hugged the baby to her. "Ssssshhhh, there," she cooed, patting Nancy's back and walking back and forth across the room, as much to calm herself as the child. It seemed like hours before her breathing gradually steadied and the shaking subsided and Annie thanked God that Nancy had woken when she did.

She knew she had to leave this place now, she was convinced of that, and there was Mary. What would she tell Mary! Fresh panic was building in her when she heard her sister's voice.

"Billy," it called. "Annie, are you there?"

Annie took a deep breath and held the quietened Nancy close. "I'm in here," she replied, "Nancy was crying, but she's fine now." Annie moved into the kitchen and presented Mary with her now smiling child.

"Where's Billy?" she asked, absently, nestling Nancy in her arms. "And weren't you going somewhere today?"

Annie bent to swing the kettle over the fire. "I think he's gone for a walk, Mary," she replied quickly. "He didn't say where." Mary seemed to accept the answer and began telling Annie about the Salvation Army meeting.

"Why don't you come along Annie?" she encouraged. "I know I've not always been as good as you about going to chapel, but this is different - you'd like it."

Mary babbled on about Captain Anderson and his wife, Isabella, but Annie's thoughts were elsewhere. Joe, she was supposed to meet Joe hours ago!

Annie needed to see him, desperately. She picked up her shawl from the double-bed, drawing her breath in sharply as she did so. "I've a message to go, Mary, "she muttered. "I promised Jessie I'd keep an eye on her two lads today, while she visited her mother in the Infirmary." For someone who had never had any need to lie, Annie was finding herself now seeming to lie about everything. If Mary had any doubts, she didn't voice them, but shrugged her shoulders in answer as she snuggled Nancy to her.

Annie ran down the stairs to the end of the close but there was no sign of Joe. She ran down William Lane and along Todburn Lane praying she would see him, to explain why she hadn't met him, but he was nowhere to be found. Despondently, she started to walk, anywhere, just so long as she didn't have to go back to William Lane and Billy Dawson.

Annie wandered aimlessly, finally finding herself knocking at Jessie Greig's door.

"Jessie!" whispered Annie as her friend appeared at the door. It was obvious to Jessie something was seriously wrong and without stopping to ask, she gathered Annie into her arms and guided her through to the kitchen. She signalled to her husband to 'get out of the way' as she eased Annie into the only armchair in the house.

"Make some tea," she instructed Eddie. "Then take the young ones out for a wee while."

Eddie eyed his two sons who had, until Annie's arrival, been happily playing a game of dominoes and indicated with his head that they should go outside and play for a while.

"The kettle's on," he muttered to Jessie, trying to ignore Annie's distress. "I'll make myself scarce then, shall I?" He coughed in embarrassment. Jessie nodded.

She handed Annie a cup of strong tea and sitting herself down on the stool beside her, waited till Annie drank the brew.

"Do you want to speak of it, Annie?" she asked gently. "You might feel better if you do."

Annie wanted to confide in her but knew the consequences to Mary if she did.

"I can't, Jessie," she murmured. "Not just now." Jessie nodded her head. "That's alright lassie, just you sit there till you feel better."

She refreshed the teapot. "Is there anythin' I can do to help, Annie?"

Annie looked at her in despair and drew a deep breath. "Things aren't going too well at home, Jessie," she began. "But I can't get my own place till I make enough money and I can't do that till I'm earning weaver's wages…"

"And you can't be a weaver till Mister Dawson says so," Jessie finished standing up and placing her hands on her hips.

"First thing tomorrow," she told Annie. "You an' me are going to see Mister Campbell."

Annie's eyes widened. "*Oh* Jessie, we *can't*, Billy will be furious."

"I think we've waited long enough for Mister Dawson to give you your own looms," she added defiantly. "Now, leave this with me." She pulled Annie to her feet. "Meet me tomorrow at the gate an' we'll see him, first thing."

Annie managed a nervous smile.

"Now, home you go, Annie Pepper and no more tears."

On Annie's return, she found Mary alone in the kitchen.

"Where have you been, Annie?" her sister demanded worriedly, "I was beginning to think something had happened to you!"

Annie was afraid to speak for fear of causing Mary any more distress.

"I'm fine, Mary," she told her. "And I've an early start tomorrow. Time for bed." She moved towards the door of her room.

"You haven't seen Billy, have you?" she asked Annie's back. "He's never been home and his dinner's ruined. It's not like him," she continued abstractly.

Annie tensed. "No Mary," she replied simply. "I haven't."

Much later that night, she heard Billy stumble in.

Annie was waiting when Jessie arrived at the mill.

"Are you sure you want to do this for me?" she asked Jessie anxiously.

Jessie nodded and led her to the door of Mr Campbell's office.

"Come in," called the deep voice, in answer to their knock.

Jessie and Annie stood before him. He looked at them quizzically.

"Well?" he asked gruffly. "I don't have all day. What is it?"

Jessie cleared her throat nervously. "It's Annie, Mister Campbell," she began, nodding towards her. "I've been teachin' her the weavin' for weeks now and she's well able for a pair o' looms of her own, but Mister Dawson won't give 'er them."

Mr Campbell leaned back in his chair.

"Mr Dawson's an overseer, Jessie. I'm sure he knows when a weaver is ready!"

Jessie coughed again. "Sure," she agreed. "You're right, but in Annie's case it's a bit different. You see, she's living with her sister, who's married to Mister Dawson and it's causing' a bit o' strife for Annie, being in the same house and all. But if she was earning weaver's pay, she'd manage to get a place of her own."

Mr Campbell digested this information. "And you say she's ready, Jessie?"

Jessie nodded enthusiastically. "Taught 'er myself," she added proudly.

Mr Campbell allowed himself a half-smile. "Leave it with me," he told them, at the same time dismissing them with a wave of his hand.

None of them spoke till they were at Jessie's looms. "Did we do the right thing, Jessie?" Annie queried anxiously.

The older woman shrugged. "If we didn't," she replied. "We'll both be out o' work before the day's over." Jessie 'knocked on' and the looms hammered into life putting an end to any further conversation.

On return from their dinner-break Billy was waiting for them.

"Follow me," he indicated to Annie. A ball of fear started running round her stomach as she walked behind him. He stopped at a pair of looms at the furthest point in the weaving flat from Jessie.

"You think you can handle them, do you?" he said, pushing the wooden handle to start the drive belt.

Annie said nothing.

"They're all yours," he continued. "Let's hope you don't regret it."

The menace in his voice frightened Annie. "Thanks, Billy," she said, her words wavering only slightly.

His eyes levelled with hers. "Don't thank me, Annie," he countered slowly. "As I said, I hope you don't live to *regret* what you did." Billy turned on his heel, leaving Annie with a feeling of foreboding.

She set the looms in motion and, as the day wore on, she forgot her nervousness over Billy in the thrill of knowing she was now a weaver and earning a weaver's pay. Towards the end of the day, despite her expertise, the shuttle jammed in its path across the warp. She looked around for Joe.

"Has anyone seen Joe the Tenter?" she called to the two weavers either side of her. They both shook their heads and one motioned her over.

"I don't think he works here anymore," she shouted. "Jean Smith said Mister Dawson sacked 'im at dinnertime."

Annie felt confusion and fear coursing through her. "Sacked!" she mouthed. The woman nodded. Just then the 'hooter' signalled the end of the day and Annie switched off her looms and ran the full length of the flat to Jessie.

"Jessie," she called anxiously. "Jessie." Her friend turned round ready to congratulate Annie on her success, but the smile faded as she saw her distress.

"Joe's been sacked!" she exclaimed near to tears.

Jessie led her outside into the yard. "Sacked, you say?" Annie nodded.

The older woman shook her head. "I don't know why he was sacked Annie, but you can be sure Mister Dawson had somethin' to do with it."

Billy had said she'd regret going to Mr Campbell, now Annie knew what he'd meant.

Mary was tidying herself as Annie returned from work. "Annie?" she asked. "Could you look after Nancy tonight for me, I've told Captain Anderson and his wife I'd help them at the Hall to arrange things for tomorrow's visit from Major Scott." Annie felt herself panic. The last thing she wanted was to be alone again with Billy.

"To tell you the truth Mary, I've not been feeling too good today, I think I've got a bit of a cold coming on and…"

"Oh, get away with you Annie," cut in Mary, still busying herself at the range. You're as strong as an ox, and Nancy'll be no bother. I'd ask Billy, but it's his night for going to the Lodge."

Annie breathed a sigh of relief. "You're right, sister," she returned quickly. "And don't worry about us, we'll both be sleepin' by the time you get back."

Mary smiled. "I won't be that late," she told her. "About half past nine or so."

She pulled on her Salvation Army bonnet and a pair of small black gloves and with a kiss for Nancy and a wave of her hand, she was out the door.

Once into the fresh air, Mary's step quickened as she turned into the Lane. She hummed a little tune to herself as she climbed the steps at the top of William Lane and crossed over Victoria Road to the Salvation Army Hall at the corner of Wellington Street.

Pushing the door open at the side of the building she entered the hall to find Captain Anderson pouring over a pile of papers and music. He looked up as he heard her enter.

"Mary," he called. "Come away in, it's good of you to help." Mary removed her bonnet and patted her hair back into place. "Why, Captain Anderson," she enthused. "You know I wouldn't let you down."

The Captain was back hunting through his papers when they began to slip off the table.

Both he and Mary made a grab for them at once, and only succeeded in tumbling the whole lot on the floor. Laughing, Mary dropped to her knees and began to pick them up. "I think I'm turning out to be more of a hindrance than a help," she told him, handing over a bundle of assorted sheet music. As she did so, Captain Anderson's hand covered hers and his eyes sought her face.

"You'll never be a hindrance to me, Mary Dawson," he said, his voice dropping to a whisper.

"Hello all," called a voice from the door, interrupting the moment. Both Mary and Captain Anderson jumped to their feet, recognising instantly that Mrs Anderson was calling them.

"Isabella!" he exclaimed. "Mary's just got here." He crossed the hall and kissed his wife on the cheek.

"And what were you two up to, John?" she teased smiling at both of them. Mary felt the colour rush to her face.

"Why nothing, Mrs Anderson," she gushed. "Just tidying the mess I made when I knocked the papers off the desk and…"

Isabella Anderson laughed. "Mary, Mary," she said. "Methinks you protest too much."

Ever since she had found Mary in Belfast that Sunday morning, all lost and alone, she'd thought Mary too lacking in the 'graces' for her own good and it had come as a great surprise to her to meet up with Mary again in Dundee where she and John Anderson had been transferred by the Salvation Army.

She had never thought of Mary as a Salvationist and was pleased when she had asked to join them, seeing it as God's wish that she kept Mary on the 'path of righteousness.'

Mary, with her musical ability, had offered to lead the Songsters at the service for Major Scott, and set about arranging the sheet music and hymns. Captain John Anderson, himself a fine pianist, had encouraged this and it was through their love of music that a rapport had developed between them.

It was no coincidence that Mary spent less and less time at home and more and more time at the hall. And since Annie came, it seemed that Billy's attentions had dwindled to nothing, justifying, in Mary's mind, the development of her other interests, including Captain Anderson.

CHAPTER 8

After Mary had gone, Annie turned her attention to Nancy. She was growing into a beautiful child with a sweet nature. Rocking her in her cradle, she couldn't help but remember her own baby and wondering sadly what had become of him. He would be a year old soon and he would never know her. Annie's eyes misted with tears and Nancy's face blurred before her. The tapping on the window didn't register at first, as her thoughts travelled through distance and time back to the Poor House and her child's birth, but as the knocking grew louder, her attention came rushing back to the present.

Annie jumped up, fearful it may be Billy, back early from the Lodge. "It can't be him," she told herself sternly. "He'd use his key." She moved tentatively to the window and pulling the curtain to one side, peeped behind it. As the chink of light shone out into the darkness a male voice called her name.

"Annie," it whispered urgently. "Annie, open the door."

Annie couldn't believe her ears. It sounded like Joe!

Letting go of the curtain, she hurried to the kitchen door. "Is that you Joe?" she called softly. "Is it you?"

"It is, Annie, quickly now, let me in."

In an instant, Joe was standing before her in the kitchen, his face tight with tension.

"Are you alright?" he demanded, looking at her intensely.

Annie nodded. "Joe, they said you've been sacked, is it true?"

"It's true Annie, your brother-in-law knows his stuff. He's been waiting for the chance to get rid of me ever since we first met and, like a fool, I gave him it. I turned in late and he sacked me on the spot."

"Oh Joe, "Annie cried. "It's all my fault."

Joe pulled her towards him. "Sssshhhh," he soothed her. "As long as you're alright. When you didn't turn up to meet me yesterday, I didn't know what to think."

The memory of Billy flashed back into her mind, but she daren't tell Joe for fear of Mary finding out. Instead she said there had been a problem with Nancy before hurrying on to tell him about getting her own looms and how soon she'd be earning enough money to leave this house.

Joe listened in silence to her news. "Are you sure you want to leave here?" he asked her. For the second time, Annie wondered if Joe knew about her and Billy, but said nothing.

"I'm sure, Joe."

"Then let me ask you something else. Do you believe in love at first sight?"

The air around felt motionless, yet every sound seemed emphasised. Her breathing, the crackle of the fire, the hiss of the gas mantel.

"Yes," she answered truthfully, for that was what had happened to her, not once, but twice. Joe took both her hands in his.

"Then, will you marry me, Annie?"

For a moment, Annie felt as if her breathing would stop entirely, but suddenly there was a rush of excitement which seemed to come from her toes and course through every bit of her body.

"I will Joe," she answered him, throwing her arms around his neck. "I will."

Nothing else mattered for some minutes as both Joe and Annie were lost in the wonderment of their love for each other.

"But Joe," Annie suddenly realised. "If Billy got rid of you, it's just as likely he'll do the same to me when he finds out and with none of us working, how can we get married?"

Once again, poverty seemed to be snatching happiness way from Annie.

Joe laughed. It was so good to see that cheeky grin again, Annie laughed too.

"That's better," he said. "Did you think I'd ask my girl to marry me if I couldn't look after her?"

Annie didn't understand. "But, you've been sacked," she began.

"Yes, I've been sacked from Baxters, but there's other things a strong bloke like me can turn his hand to. I start tomorrow, down at the docks. Yesterday, a Tenter, tomorrow a Docker," he pronounced proudly.

"But how?" Annie asked.

"Old Charlie Cassiday, me uncle on me father's side, got me the start. Spoke for me, like, told them how good I was and how strong."

Annie clasped her hands round his neck. "Oh Joe, we'll be alright then, we can get married."

The clock on the mantelpiece chimed nine making Annie realise that Mary's return was imminent. "You must go now, Joe, Mary will be back soon and I don't want her saying anything to Billy about us, not till we have to." Joe smiled.

"I know, Annie, I know." He kissed her gently full on her lips. "Everything's going to be fine now," he told her. "Just as long as you love me… by the way," he added, mischief in his eyes. "You've not told me you do! Only that you'll marry me."

She dug him in the ribs as she felt a rush of colour to her face.

Joe grinned. "Now don't you turn shy on me, Annie Pepper," he whispered, turning her face up to his. "Do you love me, Annie, like I love you?"

Annie felt as if she loved the whole world at that moment. "Yes Joe," she replied simply. "I love you with all my heart."

"Then we'll be married soon and you'll be Mrs Annie Cassiday. How d'you like the sound of that?"

Annie repeated the name to herself. "I like it fine Joe," she told him. "I like it fine. Now, you must go, before my sister returns. Annie began to push Joe in the direction of the door. "We don't want you meeting either her or Billy on the stairs, now do we?"

Joe grinned. "Be good," he whispered. "I'll see you again as soon as I can. I love you."

"And I love you too," Annie whispered. "Now *go*."

She closed the door behind him and returned to the kitchen and sweet Nancy.

"One day," she told the sleeping child. "Joe and me will have a daughter, just like you."

She bent and kissed the babe. "And one day, God willing, she'll meet her big brother."

Mary returned to find both Annie and Nancy sound asleep. There was still no sign of Billy, but that was becoming normal in the marriage. She wasn't sure which had come first, his indifference to her or her attraction to Captain John Anderson. She sang a little hymn to herself as she readied herself for bed.

"What a friend we have in Jesus…" she hummed. "All our sins and griefs to bear…"

The sound of the front door slamming ceased her singing. Quickly, she pulled the covers around her neck and closed her eyes, pretending to be asleep. She listened as Billy undressed, cursing as his drunken legs stumbled out of their trousers. The bed sagged as Billy's weight rolled onto it.

"Are you asleep, Mary?" he asked his voice slurred with alcohol and tiredness. Mary's only answer was to stir in her pretend slumber. "Sure you are," he muttered, pretending to believe her.

Annie worked hard at the mill and was soon earning her full wage. She avoided Billy as much as she could, both in the mill and at home and began to visit in secrecy, the Factor who owned the flats and rooms around the mill.

On one such Saturday afternoon visit, her persistence paid off.

"We've a single-end available Miss Pepper," the Factor advised her. "Of course, it's not much, but…"

"Where?" Annie interrupted.

Mr Brodie examined the papers in front of him. "Number five," he informed her. "William Lane."

Annie gasped. "Which one?"

Mr Brodie examined the documents again. "Low door, last house in the close."

"But that's where the Sandimans live," she told him. "Mr and Mrs Sandiman and their three bairns."

"Did live," corrected the Factor. "We had to evict them yesterday, unfortunately - non-payment of rent." His small eyes looked at her over the rim of his half-moon spectacles. "Well," he demanded. "Do you want it?"

Annie drew a deep breath and nodded. "How much?" she asked.

"Five and Tuppence a week," came the reply. "*One week in advance.*"

Annie calculated her money. "That's Ten and Fourpence," she calculated out loud. "Will you take ten shillings and I'll be owed the fourpence?"

"No," said Mr Brodie. "I'm afraid it's Ten and Fourpence or I'll offer it to someone else. There's plenty wanting a nice single-end like that one."

He pulled himself up to his full height and sniffed indignantly.

Annie counted out the full money and signed her name.

"A wise move, Miss Pepper," intoned the Factor handing her the large key. "I'm sure you'll be very happy there."

Annie slipped the key into her skirt pocket and, despite having only four shillings left to last the week, she skipped out of the Factor's office all the way up the Seagate, round into Cowgate and up St Roques Lane into King Street.

Billy was sitting morosely watching the flames in the fire when she returned.

"Where's Mary?" she asked, keeping her voice restrained.

Billy looked up. "And what do you want to know that for Annie?" he asked. "Afraid to be left alone with me?"

Annie felt her pulse quicken. "No, Billy," she answered quickly. "I only wanted to know."

She moved to pass him, but his hand caught her skirt.

"What's this?" he asked, suddenly alert. "In your pocket!"

Annie froze. She hadn't wanted Billy to know she was going until it was too late for him to stop her, but now, she had no choice but to tell him.

"A key," she answered simply. "To my own home."

Billy was suddenly on his feet. "What home?" he asked angrily. "It'd better not be with Joe Cassiday," he threatened her.

Annie stood her ground. "It's not with anyone," she shouted back. "It's just for me."

His eyes held hers in an icy glare.

"You'd better not be lying, Annie," he hissed. "'Cause if you are, I'll find out and you'll regret it. Just like you regretted going to Mr Campbell."

Annie was trembling now. "Let go, Billy," she asked shakily. "Please."

Billy released her slowly, and resumed his seat at the fire. "Get gone then, bitch," he ordered her. "And stay away from your sister too, she doesn't associate with sluts like you."

Annie ran to her room and threw herself on her bed, hurt and anger washing over her.

She had to get away, tonight. It didn't matter if she had no furniture or coal, she daren't spend another minute under the same roof as Billy.

With trembling fingers she packed her few belongings into her carpet bag and pulled her coat around her, more for comfort than against the cold. She sat very still till darkness fell and the sound of silence came from the other side of the door. Hardly daring to breathe, she opened it and crept into the kitchen. Billy was asleep in his chair, an empty whiskey bottle lying on its side by his feet. She looked at his handsome face, his strong hands and muscular arms. 'It could have all been so different,' she thought. 'But not now, not after that night.'

She gathered her skirt in front of her and tiptoed past him, out through the door and into the cold night air. Quickly, she descended the two flights of stairs to the ground floor and along the close to the end door. The key turned loosely in the lock and she entered the blackness.

The wished she'd brought a candle for light, but in her haste to leave had only brought her belongings. She could smell the recently-gone Sandimans, their collective odours permeating every corner.

Annie covered her head with her hands to blot out the darkness. It was going to be a long night.

Mary entered the kitchen clutching Nancy to her. "It's me, Billy," she called. "We're back."

Billy stirred in his chair and looked at his watch. "You're late," he told her. "It's past nine o'clock… past Nancy's bedtime." He stood up, swaying slightly, and took her from Mary's arms. "I'll see to her," he muttered, pushing open the door of the other room. He disappeared into the blackness with the baby while Mary took off her coat and bonnet and bent over the range.

"I'm making some tea," she called to Billy. "Do you want a cup?"

Billy emerged from the back room his face pale and unemotional. "Your sister's gone," he said, his voice monotone.

Mary straightened. "Gone!" she repeated. "Gone where?"

Billy looked at her, his eyes brooking no argument. "I don't know where, and I don't care. Look for yourself."

Mary rushed past him and looked into the gloom. There was no sound or movement except for Nancy's breathing. She closed the door quietly.

"Have you sent her away, Billy?" she asked, her voice even and controlled.

Billy snorted. "Sent her away, you're asking, and why should I *send* her away?"

Mary took a deep breath. "Because you can't bear to be in the same house as her and not be able to touch her."

Billy turned on her. "Touch her!" he shouted. "Is that what you think I want to do?"

Mary flinched. "Yes, Billy," she replied. "It is."

"And what would I do with her?" he spat, moving towards her. "Lie her on her back, do you think, force myself on her, eh, is that what I'd do?"

Mary felt fear forming in her breast and her heart quickened as he moved towards her.

"And me, with a beautiful wife of my own, who I can bed any time I wish… provided, *of course*, she's not praising Jesus!" Billy began pulling off her dress. "Well, how about praising *me* for a change, Mary Dawson, or don't I reach your holy standard?"

Mary closed her eyes, wishing to blot out what was to come. She felt her dress pulled from her body as Billy moved beyond control. "Annie's gone, *forever*," he cursed. "But there's always *you*, Mary, just like before."

His heavy weight bore down on top of her as tears forced their way from under her eyelids. There was no love, just lust and pain as Mary's second child was conceived.

Annie slept fitfully, cringing from shadows and jumping at noises as the house settled for the night. It was cold and damp as she huddled in the corner. The life in Dundee she had embraced with fervour had suddenly turned against her. The only thing she could be sure of was that tomorrow would dawn. Long before it did, she was wide awake, pacing the floor to keep warm. She had four shillings left from her wages to keep her till Friday and she prayed that Billy wouldn't sack her as he'd sacked Joe, for without work, she would be destitute again. She drank from the cold tap and pulled her shawl around her. It was half past six in the morning as she closed the door behind her and headed for the Mill. Praying Billy wouldn't notice her, she hid behind the stone pillar holding the iron gate into Baxters yard and waited for Jessie to arrive. At seven o'clock, Jessie came by.

"Jessie," she hissed from her hiding place. Jessie turned sharply and squinted into the shadow.

"Annie?" she asked hesitantly. "Is that you?"

Annie pulled her into the greyness. "I've left them," she told Jessie. "Billy and Mary, I've left them."

Jessie nodded. "An' where are you staying?" she asked, concern in her voice.

"I've got a place in William Lane, just down the stairs from Mary, but it's mine, Jessie, it's mine."

Jessie smiled. "Well done, Annie. What did Mister Dawson and your sister say when you told them?"

Annie shivered. "That's just it, Jessie, they don't know where I am and they mustn't find out either." Jessie looked confused. "It's a long story, Jessie," she continued. "But I need to tell someone where I am, and I want it to be you."

Jessie hugged her. "Your secret's safe wi' me," she whispered. "Now, come on, time we were workin', you can tell me all about it at dinner-time."

Annie worked feverishly all morning and at the sound of the 'bummer' hastened outside to meet Jessie. She told her that the Factor had offered her a house in William Lane on Saturday and she'd taken it on the spot. It had left her almost penniless but for four shillings and sixpence, but she would make do till Friday when she would have her weaver's wage.

"I'll no ask the real reason for your leavin' 'cause I don't think I want to know, but if it's alright with you, me an' the bairns'll drop in to see you the night with one or two wee things that might make your week a bit easier to bear."

Annie felt overwhelming gratitude to Jessie. She had barely known her a few months, but she had risked her job for her and now, she was risking the wrath of Billy if he found out she'd befriended her.

"There's no one I'd rather have as my first visitor," Annie said. "Just mind how you go and watch out for Billy."

Jessie nodded and the two friends returned to their looms.

That night, Jessie knocked at Annie's door carrying a basket and followed by her two sons.

She produced candles and coal, bread and tea and a heavy crocheted blanket.

"That'll keep you goin',"she told Annie. "You can pay me back when you're on your feet."

Annie lit the candles and the boys made up a fire and before long the little house was warming in the flickering light. The old kettle which hung on an iron hook over the fire was filled with water and Annie tipped in some tea. Empty jars left by the Sandimans were pressed into service as cups and the bread which Jessie had brought was shared between them. It was the finest meal Annie had tasted and hope returned to her spirits.

"I'll never forget your kindness, Jessie," she told her friend. "And I'll pay you back tenfold," she promised as she bade her goodnight.

The candle spluttered and failed as Annie pulled the blanket around her.

"It's going to be alright," she told herself closing her eyes. "It's going to be alright."

Billy went to work earlier than usual, leaving Mary in a silent heap in bed. She listened as he washed and shaved at the kitchen sink, her senses heightened and tense in case he wanted her again. But the front door banged shut and he was gone. Mary swung her legs over the edge of the bed just as uncontrolled sobbing overtook her. The tension of the night before and the thought of what life would now be like in the future suddenly overwhelming her.

Her sobbing woke Nancy and she hurried through to her.

"Oh, Nancy," she whispered to the child. "What's to become of us now?" Nancy gurgled with joy in the arms of her mother and Mary hugged her closer.

It was all her fault, she told herself. She'd been the one who'd wanted Annie to come and live with them. She'd insisted Billy found work for her sister at the mill and now, she had lost both of them.

By the time she had fed Nancy, her tears of sorrow were being replaced by guilt. She must find Annie. If Billy knew where she was he wasn't going to tell her, she was sure of that. She would ask Captain Anderson's advice, she decided. He'd know what to do. Thinking of John Anderson made Mary feel warm again and, hurriedly, she dressed Nancy and herself. By mid-morning she was making her way to the Captain's house in Victoria Road.

Captain Anderson greeted her with a surprised smile. "Why, Mary," he said. "I didn't expect to see you this early. Isabella's not in I'm afraid, she's out visiting an old Army Officer who's not been too well lately." He ushered her in. "But come away in Mary and the beautiful Nancy."

Mary could smell lavender and camphor. Everything in the wide hallway shone, the floor, the mirror, the hat stand. "Follow me," instructed the Captain. Mary walked behind him, Nancy perched on her arm. An awareness that they were alone in the house drifted through her consciousness. She sat Nancy on the carpet and herself on a small wooden chair beside her. Captain Anderson indicated an armchair to her. "You'll be more comfortable there, Mary," he told her. "Would you like some tea perhaps?"

"No, no thanks, I wanted to ask for your help actually." Mary hung her head.

Captain Anderson fought down an urge to rush over to her. "What's wrong?" he asked quietly, holding his ground.

Mary took a deep breath. "It's Annie, my sister," she began. "She's disappeared."

"Disappeared? What do you mean, Mary, people don't just disappear."

Mary pulled a handkerchief from the pocket of her skirt. She raised her eyes, blue and tearful to meet his.

"When I got back from the Hall on Sunday, Billy was in a black mood. I've never seen him like that before." She dabbed her eyes and sniffed. John Anderson felt every muscle in his body tense as he watched her small frame bowed before him. "When I asked him what was wrong, he just said that Annie had gone and I wasn't to see her ever again…" Genuine tears of confusion and hurt soaked her handkerchief.

John Anderson could stand it no longer. He crossed the room and knelt beside her, taking her small hand in his. "Mary, Mary," he whispered. "Please don't be upset, we'll find Annie for you, trust me. I'll not rest till you're reunited with her."

Nancy squealed in delight having found a cord tassel holding back the curtains at the window.

John Anderson released Mary's hand and jumped to his feet. His whole body was aching with secret desire for her. "We'd better go," Mary said her voice trembling from the sudden heat of the encounter, to which she too, was a party.

"C'mon Nancy," she said, bending to lift her child. "Time for your dinner."

John Anderson caught her arm as she passed by him to the door. She stopped instantly.

He wanted to say so much to her but could not. "I'll do everything I can to find her Mary. I can do no more," he added, trying to convey to her his frustration.

Mary could say nothing, her voice having deserted her, but her eyes told him, she too, could do no more.

CHAPTER 9

Billy watched for Annie to arrive at her looms. His feelings for her had not diminished since their last encounter but were, in fact, becoming obsessional. The image of Joe Cassiday touching her fuelled his hatred of him and his determination that Joe would never have Annie.

The minute hand on the mill clock moved to seven. She'd be starting soon and he'd see her again. Annie was waiting outside the weaving flat till seconds before the hour before going in.

The looms had already started their deafening clatter as she knocked on, keeping her head down and her eyes on the shuttles.

Billy knew it was useless to try to talk to her just now, but at least, she was still under his control as long as she worked at the mill and that was enough in the meantime.

At break times she stuck close to Jessie.

"Can I ask you yet another favour Jessie?" she enquired anxiously of her friend. "I know I don't deserve any more help from you, you've done enough…"

"God lassie," Jessie interrupted. "You know if I can do anythin' for you, I'll do it. You just have to ask."

Annie felt her shoulders relax. "Tell Joe," she said. "Tell him where I am and to come and see me. But tell him to be careful, Jessie. There's no telling what Billy will do if he finds out where I am."

Jessie laughed. "You mean he doesn't know you're livin' just below him?"

Annie nodded. "Sometimes the best place to hide is close by and it means I'm still near to Mary, just in case she needs me."

"I'll send one o' the bairns down to the docks with a message when they finish at dinner-time the morrow. Write a wee note the night an' I'll make sure he gets it." Jessie patted her hand. "C'mon, back to the toil." She smiled. "Hard work never killed anybody, it just feels like it somtimes."

Jessie was as good as her word and the following day sent her eldest son, Jimmy, off to the docks with the note. He waited for Joe at the dock gate and pestered the other dockers to point him out.

"Are you Joe Cassiday?" he asked Joe.

"I am, and what's it to a lad like you?"

"I've a note for you. My ma says I've to make sure you get it."

"And who's your ma?" Joe asked.

"Jessie," replied the boy. "Jessie Greig."

Joe fished in his pocket and handed Jimmy a penny.

Jimmy beamed. "Thanks mister."

"Thank you," said Joe, grinning. "Now make sure you go straight home."

Joe unfolded the note.

'Dear Joe,' it read, 'I've found a place to live and must speak with you. Don't let Billy see you.'

It gave the address and was signed, 'Your love, Annie.'

Joe pushed the note into his pocket. He'd go to her that night. Rain began to fall as he hurried home to the room he shared with his brother and by the time he got there, he was soaked through.

Charlie was coaxing the fire into life.

"Fetch some coal," he called over his shoulder. "This bloody fire'll never light."

Joe opened the lid of the wooden coal bunker at the sink and shovelled the black fuel into a small bucket.

Charlie was older than him and took everything in life very seriously, especially his responsibility towards his younger brother.

"You're soaked," he exclaimed, throwing the coal onto the back of the smoking grate. "You'll give yourself bloody pneumonia so you will."

Joe grinned. "Not before I marry Annie, I won't," he retorted, slapping Charlie on the shoulders. "and I'm seeing her tonight."

"I'll pray for you at Mass then, you'll need it getting involved with a relative of Billy Dawson."

Joe frowned at the memory of Billy. "She's not a relative, she's just his sister-in-law and anyway, she's left home," he told Charlie. "I've a note from her." He showed his brother the piece of paper.

Charlie read it and handed it back. "Careful, Joe," he warned. "You can never trust these Ulstermen."

"You mean Dawson?"

"I mean Dawson, Joe. He's not exactly got a liking for us Catholics. He made that wife of his change religion before he married her and it wasn't a full nine months after the marriage that she gave birth neither."

"Get away with you, Charlie. You're getting like an old fishwife."

Charlie shrugged. "Just watch your step, Joe, low morals usually run in families."

Joe threw the warm water over himself as he washed away the sweat of the day at the small sink. "My Annie's not like her sister," he told Charlie. "She's a good Catholic girl. Now, let's hear no more of your babbling."

Making sure no one was around and with only the light from the gas mantle at the end of the close showing him the way, Joe crept along the narrow flagged walkway to the end door.

There was no light showing and he wondered if he had found the right place. He tapped softly on the door. "Annie," he hissed. "It's me, Joe."

There was a faint movement from inside and the scrape of a key turning in the lock. Annie's face appeared out of the darkness, her eyes scouring the space surrounding Joe.

"Are you alone?"

"Don't be daft, Annie, let me in."

She closed the door quietly behind him and allowed her breathing to return to normal. "Oh Joe, I'm so glad to see you." They held each other for a few moments, allowing the tension to ebb before releasing one another.

Joe looked around the gloom. A small candle burned in a saucer on the floor and apart from that, there was no furniture in the room at all.

"Annie," Joe exclaimed. "You can't live like this."

"It's alright," she assured him. "It's just till I get my wages on Friday, then I'll go to the market and pick up some bits and pieces."

He pulled her towards him. "Oh, Annie, this is all my fault."

"No, Joe, it's not your fault and you mustn't think like that. I love you and if this is the only way we can see one another, then so be it." She didn't say it was due to Billy's assault on her that she had left as quickly as she had. It would only have led to more questions which she didn't want to answer.

"I'll get you some things," Joe told her. "There's plenty of men at the docks who know how to lay hands on furniture and stuff cheaply. Leave it with me."

Annie lay her head against his shoulder. "Just hold me, Joe, and I'll be alright. Just hold me."

The flickering candle cast their shadows onto the grimness of the walls around them.

"Will you still marry me, Annie?" Joe whispered. "Even though I've brought you to this?"

Annie could feel the strength of Joe's arms around her and pulled her shoulders back. "I'll marry you Joe, when the time's right and I'll make you the finest wife that ever lived."

A mixture of pride and determination surged through Joe's heart. "And I'll make you the finest husband," he replied. "Now, try to get some rest and leave everything else to me."

Joe squeezed her hand and kissed her before quietly leaving the little house. "Goodnight my love, I'll see you again soon."

"Goodnight Joe," Annie replied. "Remember I love you."

Mary was becoming more depressed. Each day her thoughts were filled with images of Captain John Anderson and the futility of ever truly knowing him and each day, too, the distance between her and Billy widened, until it had become a black hole between them, through which she was now in danger of dropping.

He still refused to have Annie's name mentioned in the house and although she knew he was somehow to blame for her sudden departure, her fear of him was now so heightened that she daren't broach the subject.

Her only source of happiness was Nancy. "One day," she told her, gazing at the gurgling child, "You'll be a beautiful young woman and men will come calling on you to ask your hand in marriage and you'll live happily…" Mary's voice faltered. How her own dreams had crumbled.

Suddenly, she caught sight of herself in the mirror above the mantelpiece and walked towards the image. Her clear skin and blue eyes were dull and lifeless. Small lines furrowed her forehead and the corners of her mouth drooped. "Look at yourself, Mary Dawson," she murmured. "What happened to the girl you were?" As she stared at her sad reflection, the fighting spirit which had deserted her cautiously began to reawaken. She pulled herself upright and lifted her chin, forcing a smile to begin. "No-one's going to deny me happiness," she told her reflection firmly. "Not Billy nor anyone else."

She turned to Nancy and picked her up, kissing her black curls. "C'mon my lovely one," she murmured. "We're going out."

It was a bright day, and as they walked through the town, Mary's spirits continued to lift. She noticed people smiling at her and Nancy as they passed by and she found herself smiling back. She bought herself some new ribbons for her hair at the haberdashers in the Wellgate.

There was nothing she could do to change Billy or her feelings for John Anderson, but she could do something about her sister and despite Billy's warnings, she was determined to find her. Somehow, her footsteps took her up the Wellgate steps onto Victoria Road and the Army Hall. The door was ajar and inside she could hear a voice raised in anger.

She stopped and listened. "And I tell you now," said a female voice. "If there's any more talk about you and her, then you'll be finished in the Army. Neither Jesus Christ nor Major Scott condone adultery." Mary shrank back into the shadows of the vestibule as the figure of Isabella Anderson swept past. Hardly daring to breathe, she tiptoed back to the door and looked into the hall. It was empty. Whoever Isabella was angry with had gone.

She waited a few moments then made her way back home. It was unlike Isabella to shout at anyone, whoever had been on the receiving end of her anger must have upset her badly and there was only one person who could have done that, Mary reasoned. Isabella's husband, John.

Her mind was racing. Had someone noticed her looking at him with longing in her eyes and told Isabella, or had something been said by John himself. Perhaps he was in love with someone else, but that someone else wasn't her. Her bravado suddenly deserted her again as fear once more took over. It was all turning back into the nightmare from which she now seemed incapable of wakening.

Friday eventually came round and Annie collected her wages. Fourteen shillings and sixpence. She counted the money into her purse and holding her shawl tightly round her, carefully made her way home. She lit her last candle and pulled the curtains closed. Her meagre meal consisted of porridge which she cooked in a small pot on the fire and which she ate ravenously. Had it not been for the goodness of Jessie, once more, sharing her lowly rations with her she would have gone hungry.

As she huddled down in her makeshift bed by the fire thinking of what she would buy the next day to try to make her room more habitable, the silence was broken by a loud banging at the door. Annie froze. She'd thought she'd been so careful. Could Billy possibly have found out she was here!

Perhaps if she kept perfectly still, he'd go away. The banging started again. Annie's heart was pounding but there was nothing for it but to answer the door and get it over with.

One thing she was sure of, no matter how angry Billy was, she wasn't going back, no matter what he said or did.

Steeling herself for the conflict, she flung open the door.

In front of her stood a huge, red-faced man, a bonnet pulled over one eye and carrying a table on his head.

He grinned and leaned towards her. "Joe sent me," he whispered, winking. Annie gulped and stood back as he crushed past her ducking to avoid the table hitting the door lintel.

"I suppose you want this anywhere?" he asked looking around the empty room. Annie nodded.

"Don't close the door just yet," he added winking. "There's more."

He returned with two chairs and a bed frame. "You'll have to find your own covers." He smiled. "But at least you've got something to put them on now."

With a whispered, "Cheerio missus," he was gone.

Annie bumped down on one of the chairs and looked at the furniture in amazement.

Joe had been true to his word. A warm glow filled her with new strength.

"There's no going back now, Annie," she told herself. "From now on this is home."

The following day, Annie and Jessie, with her two sons in tow as carriers, took themselves down town to the flea market in the Overgate.

"You'll need bedclothes, pots and a dish or two," advised Jessie, thoroughly enjoying the shopping spree. "I've only got five shillings to spend on the lot," Annie reminded her friend, but Jessie brushed her protests aside. "You've got *ten shillin's?*" she told her. "Five of your own an' five of mine."

"Oh, Jessie," Annie smiled. "If I live to be a hundred, I'll never know kindness like you've shown me."

Jessie glowed and her eyes misted. "Well, Annie, like I said, if you were my daughter…" she sniffed loudly. "C'mon," she continued. "Start rummagin'."

All afternoon they squirrelled amongst the piles of second-hand goods spread in rows on the cobbles, finally settling on a large quilt, a feather pillow, two pots, a frying pan and an assortment of crockery and cutlery.

Jessie, Annie and the two boys staggered home laden with their purchases.

They giggled and tripped and giggled again but nothing could diffuse Annie's exuberance as they turned into the Lane, she had even forgotten Billy and her fear of him.

Mary woke early on Sunday morning and taking care not to rouse the sleeping Billy, she got herself ready for the ten o'clock service at the Army Hall. Usually Annie looked after Nancy while she was gone and she wondered if she should take the child with her.

As she was deciding, Billy's voice sounded in her ears.

"Praising Jesus again, are we?" he asked sarcastically.

Mary tensed. "Will you mind Nancy, or do you want me to take her with me?" she asked, trying to ignore his remark.

The bedsprings creaked as Billy turn over. "Do what you want," he muttered.

"I'll leave her then," Mary replied. There was no answer.

Mary slipped on her bonnet and coat, picked up her bible and, closing the door quietly behind her, stepped out into the Sunday morning air. But she was not the only one taking the air. Annie was watching her go. Quickly closing the door behind her, she followed Mary, at a distance, to the hall. Once the service was over, she had decided, she would speak with her, tell her where she was and mend the broken bridge that lay between them, due to Billy.

Mary joined the other Salvationists as they filed into the hall. Isabella and John Anderson greeted her at the door. She tried to sense any difference in Isabella's greeting, but found none, but it was different with the Captain.

"Welcome Mary," he smiled at her, holding her hand tighter than necessary. Mary felt herself colour and quickly looked to see if Isabella had noticed. She hadn't. "There's a problem with the Songsters," he told her. "Perhaps you could remain after the service to discuss it." Mary felt her heartbeat quicken.

"Of course," she replied too quickly. "After the service then." John Anderson reluctantly let go of her hand.

The service seemed endless, but eventually it was over. Mary busied herself amongst the song sheets and music beside the organ till the hall emptied and only herself and John Anderson remained.

He stood tall in front of her. "I need to speak to you about something Mary." His voice sounded strained.

"Yes, the Songsters," Mary replied. "There's a problem?"

John looked at his feet and clasped his hands behind his back. "It's not the Songsters, Mary, I need to speak to you about something more… personal." Mary felt rooted to the spot. "But not here," he continued. "Is there somewhere we could talk?"

Mary felt the weight of the decision on her shoulders and it was too heavy for her.

She shrugged her shoulders to release the tension. "Can't it be said here?" she asked, wanting desperately to know what he had to say but fearing the knowledge at the same time.

"Better not," he replied, nodding his head. "Come with me to the house," he asked her. "I must speak with you urgently."

Mary was becoming more and more agitated as the intrigue continued. She knew she wanted John Anderson, more than anything in the world, but she also knew they were both married and, to make matters worse, he was a Captain in the Salvation Army.

"My husband will be expecting me home soon," she said, not knowing why she said it.

At the mention of the word husband, John Anderson seemed to lose control of the situation.

His hands cupped themselves round Mary's face. In a silence which could be felt, John Anderson kissed her. Mary let herself go into his embrace, everything else forgotten in that moment.

"I love you," he said simply. "God help me Mary, but I love you."

Annie quietly slipped back through the hall doorway and out into the street.

This wasn't the time to reappear to her sister. She had meant to surprise her after the service and tell her all that had happened, but now, now it was different. Their reunion would have to wait.

CHAPTER 10

Annie busied herself for the rest of the day, cleaning and arranging her bits and pieces about her. She was feeling increasingly relaxed now and looking forward to seeing Joe that evening. Billy, far from being an object of fear, now became almost one of pity. She knew how it felt to find out the one you loved was loving someone else and, sooner or later, Billy was going to find out too.

Not for the first time, she marvelled at Mary's courage and began to feel that, together, they could stand up to Billy and find their own happiness without him. All sorts of images and plans were flitting through her mind when she heard Joe's knock at the door.

He smiled and bowed as she opened the door. "A gentleman caller for Miss Pepper," he announced. Annie giggled and pulled him inside.

"Come and look," she begged. "Thank you, Joe, for everything."

Joe felt a warm love for Annie spread through his body. "It'll do till we're wed," he told her, lifting her chin with his finger so that he could kiss her more easily.

"Will we be wed soon, Joe?"

He nodded. "Sooner than you think, Annie. In fact," he pulled her down beside him on her little bed. "I don't see why we don't tie the knot before Christmas."

Annie blinked. "But that's only… nine weeks from now."

"And how many weeks does my Annie want to make me wait for her?"

He rolled her on the bed onto her back and pulled her close to him.

"And how long do you think I can wait to make love to my virgin bride?"

Annie felt her blood run cold. She pushed Joe off her, trying to mask her nervousness by feigning embarrassment. "Why Joe Cassiday, I'll have no more talk like that till after our wedding. Now, sit up and I'll make us some tea."

Joe held his hands up in submission. "Anything you say, my love, but one more kiss before you go near that kettle." He swung Annie round to face him. "I'll put the bans up tomorrow," he said softly, kissing her cheeks, her eyes and her lips. "And three weeks from now you'll be Mrs Annie Cassiday, my wife."

Annie nodded, the joy draining from her as she wondered how she was going to tell Joe about Billy and their baby son in Ireland.

Billy was becoming more and more morose. Every day he watched Annie arrive at her loom and wondered where she had spent the night. His moods when he was with Mary were deepening into darkness, at once he was glad he had her and, for sure, he loved his daughter, Nancy, but at the same time, his dreams were of Annie.

Her avoidance of him only fuelled his jealousy of Joe Cassiday and thoughts of them, together, constantly invaded his consciousness. He took to drinking more and more at nights, to avoid returning to his home without her and it was on such a night that he decided Joe Cassiday would be dealt with, once and for all.

The lights from the Thrums Bar cast a yellow gleam over Billy as he steadied himself on the pavement outside. His feet turned up King Street, towards Todburn Lane, but as fate would have it, he met Joe walking towards the bar for a late drink with his brother Charlie.

Billy barred their way. "So, we meet again, do we?" he slurred. "The great Joe Cassiday himself."

"You're drunk," stated Joe making to pass him by, but Billy lurched in front of him.

"Not so fast, Mister, I want a word with you."

Joe turned to his brother. "I'll see you in the pub in a while, Charlie," he told him, patting him in the shoulder to reassure him he was handling things.

Charlie nodded reluctantly and walked away.

Joe leaned against the end of a dark close which led to the back lands of King Street.

"Will up here do you, Mister Dawson?" The emphasis on Mister did nothing to calm Billy's mind as he walked past Joe into the gloom.

Joe followed, lighting a cigarette and blowing the smoke into the night air as he watched for Billy's next move.

"Are you bedding her?" Billy asked into the silence.

Joe inhaled deeply. "That's none of your business, Billy Dawson."

Billy asked again, this time with a cold anger which had welled inside him.

A grin crossed Joe's face. "Jealous, are you, Billy? Greedy for what you can't have?"

"I've had her before you," Billy suddenly erupted. "And I'll have her again, once you're out of the way."

Joe didn't see the blow coming and it caught him full on the jaw.

His head hit the wall of the close, then the flagstones beneath his feet, as he fell in a heap with Billy on top of him.

"Stay away from her," Billy spat through clenched teeth. "She's mine."

Joe fought to push him off, his head bleeding and his senses dazed. "*Liar*," he shouted, forcing Billy on to his side. "Annie wouldn't lie with scum like you. She's a lady and she's going to be my wife." Tears began to burn in Joe's eyes. "My *wife*, do you hear, you bastard, my *wife*."

The drink had turned Billy's limbs to jelly and his arms flailed the night air to no avail. "*Ask her*," he shouted into the darkness. "*Ask her*."

Joe struggled to his feet. "Stay away from me Billy Dawson," he hissed. "And from Annie, or so help me, I'll kill you."

Billy rolled onto his back and stared at the stars above him through the ropes of limp washing hanging like ghosts in the blackness. "Annie," he whispered. "It wasn't meant to be like this." Hot tears of spent anger coursed down his face.

"Are you alright, Mister?"

The white face of a street urchin was peering down at him.

Billy sniffed and pulled himself upright, motioning for the child to go away.

"Do you want me to fetch anybody?"

He grasped the boy's arm and pulled himself to his feet. "No, thanks," he muttered. "Now away home with you, you should be in your bed." He searched in his pocket for a penny. "Here." He pushed the penny into the boy's hand. "And don't you tell anyone what you saw, do you hear me?"

The white face nodded and disappeared.

Billy leant against the lime washed wall of the close and tried to still the turmoil in his soul.

He had tried so hard to make everything right, marrying Mary and giving her child his name. And Mary had wanted her sister to come here so much, he couldn't refuse, nor had he wanted to. But no matter how much he searched for peace it wasn't to be found and, eventually, he returned home.

The kitchen clock ticked the measured passing of time and the glow from the dying embers of the fire illuminated Mary asleep in their bed. He untied his shoes and hung his jacket on the chair back.

Mary stirred. "Billy," she called softly. "Is that you?"

"It's me."

"Are you alright?"

Billy grunted. "Go to sleep, Mary," he told her. "I'll be coming to bed soon."

But that night and for many nights to come, Billy slept in Annie's bed in the back room.

The blood was drying on Joe's face as he knocked at Annie's door.

He could hear her move about inside and knew she was still awake.

"Annie," he called as loud as he dare. "Open the door."

"Is that you Joe?"

"Open the door," he repeated more urgently. "I'm hurt."

The bolt drew back and Annie's head appeared, her face white with concern. Panic began to well inside her at the sight of Joe's bloodied face. Her hand reached out to touch him but he grasped it with his own, forcing her inside and closing the door behind him.

"Joe," she asked, the anxiety filling her vocal chords with vibration. "What happened?"

He sat down on the edge of the bed. "Get me a cloth."

Annie ran to the sink and rinsed cold water onto a towel and sitting beside him she began to dab at the cut. "What happened?"

"I've had a run-in with your brother-in-law. That's what's happened."

Annie felt a wave of fear wash through her. "Billy?" she asked weakly.

Joe nodded and turned to face her. "He said a strange thing, Annie."

Annie stared at him, her breathing seeming to have deserted her. "And what was that?" she asked, dreading the answer.

Joe's shoulders slumped and his eyes fixed on the toes of his boots. "He said he was glad you no longer lived with him and Mary, that you were not to be trusted."

Annie flinched.

Joe continued. "He said you were a bad lot, Annie. Can you imagine anyone saying that about you?"

Annie felt a calm descend upon her. Joe knew. "I slept with him, Joe… twice."

His hands clenched into fists as the words hit his heart. "So he said."

Annie sat on the chair opposite him. "He's my uncle's stepson, Joe, he came to help with the harvest, back home in Ireland."

Joe's eyes remained focused on the floor. "I fell in love with him, almost in an instant," Annie continued. "He promised to marry me and that we'd be together in Scotland but…" Her voice faltered. "Oh, Joe," she whispered. "I'm sorry."

"And how did Mary come into this sorry tale?" he asked still staring at his boots.

Annie inhaled deeply. "She was pregnant to him, I believe."

"Have you reason to doubt it was his?"

"No."

Joe nodded. "So he seduced you and then your sister."

It was Annie's turn to hang her head. "So it would seem," she said quietly.

He lifted his head and Annie could see the tears streaming down his face.

She made to move towards him but Joe stopped her with a raised hand.

"Don't talk anymore," he told her. "I've heard enough." He stood up and moved towards the door.

"Don't go, Joe," Annie pleaded, as the pain of guilt engulfed her. "Don't go."

He turned to face her. "Will you marry me?" he asked suddenly.

Annie's heart leapt in disbelief. "Even though you know I'll not be your virgin bride?"

"Even though," he repeated.

Annie wanted to throw herself into his arms, but, somehow, could not. She stepped back instead of forward. Some inner voice warned her that something was wrong.

"Do you mean it?" she asked, her head held high and her heart pounding.

Joe began to laugh, at first softly, but then almost hysterically, his laughter mixing with the tears which still ran down his face.

"Imagine Joe Cassiday being caught out by a bloody weaver," he shouted. "Why, you had me fooled good and proper Annie Pepper. I almost believed you were the love of my life."

Annie backed into the shadows of the small kitchen.

Joe's arms waved in resignation. "Don't worry, Annie," he assured her through his tears. "I won't seduce you. *I loved you, Annie Pepper*, but not now… not now."

Her whole body shook with emotion but guilt made Annie powerless to do anything. "Perhaps you should go now," she murmured, holding back the wave of hurt that was threatening to envelope her.

For what seemed like an eternity the silence hung between them. Then, Joe nodded. "Perhaps I should Annie, perhaps I should." He silently closed the door, as Annie fell onto her bed in a heap of misery.

Billy had won. Despite all her efforts to break free and make a life for herself, he had ruined it all. Her small room blurred into a watery prison as she sobbed herself to sleep.

Mary brushed the whiteness from Billy's jacket. "Your jacket's in a right state," she said. "All chalk like."

Billy pulled the coat from her hand. "It's lime, from the close in King Street," he told her. "I had too much to drink last night and… well, you know what drink does to you."

Mary nodded, retrieving the garment. "I'll brush it for you, shall I?"

Billy watched her as she swept the coat clean.

"At that Salvation Army Hall again tonight, are you?" he asked morosely.

Mary tensed. "It's Songsters practice," she lied brightly. "Mrs Anderson and me are putting them through their paces tonight for Sunday."

Billy grunted and snatched the jacket from her.

"Just make sure Nancy's alright," he told her, glowering.

"I will, Billy, "she assured him. "You know I wouldn't do anything to harm our Nancy."

"Maybe you should find that sister of yours," he muttered. "Get her to come back."

Mary put the brush onto the table. "You mean you'd let her back in Billy?" she asked, her heart lifting in joy.

Her husband nodded. "If she's sorry," he added. "Really sorry."

Mary nodded. "I'll see if I can find her, Billy. Someone must know where she is!"

Billy pulled on the coat and picked up his mill keys.

"I'll be home at six tonight. Make sure me tea's ready."

Mary nodded. "Yes Billy, six o'clock it is." Billy left the kitchen and Mary twirled herself round in a delighted circle. "Annie's coming home," she told Nancy. "If we can find her."

Mary sang to herself as she dressed Nancy and popped her into her pram.

John Anderson was waiting for her and the sooner she told him of the change in Billy's attitude towards Annie the quicker he could find her and bring her back.

With Annie there, she would be free to go to John whenever she wanted, safe in the knowledge that Billy would be looked after by Annie.

Mary was no fool. She had seen the way Billy had looked at her sister all too often and now she had found true love with John Anderson, she felt no jealousy, only the desire that Billy would give her an excuse to leave him.

John Anderson was waiting in the deserted hall and turned quickly at the sound of the door creaking open.

"It's only me," whispered Mary into the dim interior. John held out his arms to welcome her.

"You're here at last," he whispered. "I was so afraid you'd forgotten."

"Forgotten?" echoed Mary. "Never." They held each other in the stillness and marvelled at the love they had found in each other.

"It's dangerous here, Mary," John murmured. "Come with me to the house, to the bedroom and let me love you."

Mary felt weak with longing for him. Silently, he took her hand and led her to his home.

Lovemaking with Billy was quick and loveless but with John it was slow and warm, every fibre of her body felt languid and heavy as he stroked away her guilt-tinged resistance.

"I love you," he murmured into her hair. "Forever."

Their passion exhausted, Mary lay in John's arms, limply watching the rise and fall of his breathing.

"Will we ever be together?" she asked.

John pulled her into him. "Yes," he replied simply. "If it's God's will."

On her return home that night, Annie was waiting at the end of the close to meet her.

Mary squinted into the shadows cast by the street lamp onto a small figure.

"Annie," she called out in disbelief. "Is that you?"

Annie stepped into the light. "It's me, Mary, come to see you."

Mary whooped with delight and ran to hug her. "I knew you'd come back," she beamed. "I just knew it."

Annie laughed at her child-like optimism. "I haven't been far away," she told Mary. "Come, follow me."

Mary followed her sister along the dark walkway to the end door. "Who lives here?" she asked.

Annie turned the key in the lock. "Why, Mary, I live here."

Mary followed her into the small kitchen and waited while she lit a candle. Her eyes widened in amazement at the small, neat room, furnished sparsely, but furnished nonetheless.

"But *how*?"

Annie guided her to the chair. "Sit here," she ordered. "And I'll make us some tea."

She busied herself with the kettle and the cups, while Mary caught her breath.

"All the time," Mary marvelled. "You've been here all the time?"

Annie nodded. "I wanted to be close to you, but not to Billy, so when the chance came to take this place, I did."

At the mention of Billy's name, Mary seemed to shrink. "He wants you to come back," she whispered. "Says I've to find you and ask you to come back."

Annie handed her the cup of tea. "I'll never come back Mary, not while he's there."

Mary leant forward in the chair. "But, Annie, I want you to come back, and so does Nancy, she misses you so!"

Annie turned and faced her. "And what about John Anderson, does he miss me too?"

Mary shot back into the chair. "John Anderson," she replied, her voice rising in panic. "How do you know of John Anderson?"

Annie knelt down beside her and took her hand. "I came to the hall one night, to see you, to tell you where I was, and you were there with him. Mary, it was obvious you weren't just friends."

Mary felt the blood drain from her face. "Don't tell Billy, Annie, please, please, don't tell Billy."

"SSShhhhh," comforted Annie. "Nobody's going to tell Billy anything, but just don't get me involved in what's going on between you and Captain Anderson."

"Oh, Annie," Mary whimpered, the tears beginning to drop onto her skirt. "It's been awful since you left. Billy doesn't come home anymore, and when he does, he sleeps in Nancy's room and I don't know what's to become of me…"

Annie stroked her hand. "Nothing's going to become of you Mary, not while I'm here."

"But Billy says you've to come home… oh, Annie, please come home."

"*No,*" Annie replied emphatically. "I'll do everything I can to help, but I'll not live under the same roof as Billy Dawson."

"Shall I tell him where you are?"

Annie considered her answer. "He'll find out sooner or later, I suppose," she said. "And I'd sooner he found out from you than anyone else."

Mary nodded, drying her tears. "But what about Joe Cassiday?" she asked panicking again.

Annie felt her chin quiver. "Joe won't be coming round anymore," she said. "Don't ask any more questions now, Mary, just go home and know I'm here for you if you need me."

The two sisters hugged in the candlelight.

"It wasn't meant to be like this, was it?" whispered Mary.

Annie smiled. "No, Mary," she said. "It wasn't."

Mary crept quietly into her house hoping Billy was asleep, but he was waiting for her.

He was looking at his pocket watch as she entered the room.

"It's gone nine," he told her. "Where have you been?"

Mary drew a deep breath. "With my sister."

Billy tipped his head to one side and glanced at her from the corner of one eye. "Annie?"

Mary nodded. "She's not coming back Billy, but I know where she's living and it's not far."

Billy motioned her towards him. "Where?"

Mary stepped forward. "Downstairs," she announced triumphantly. "She's living in the Sandimans old house at the end of the close."

Billy sat back in his chair, allowing the feeling of elation and relief to wash over him. "Alone?"

Mary nodded. "Seems her and Joe Cassiday have parted company, but don't ask me why, she wouldn't say."

Billy felt a smile pull at his lips. She was his again, his alone. "Time for bed," he announced, moving towards the back room. "See you in the morning."

Mary was left standing alone in the kitchen. "Yes," she whispered. "See you in the morning."

CHAPTER 11

It was two weeks later before Mary realised something was amiss and a further two weeks before she was sure she was pregnant. She furiously tried to recount the days to determine when, and with whom, the conception had taken place and, no matter how much she tried to move the dates, she finally had to admit that it could only be Billy's child.

This realisation was both a blessing and a dread. Billy no longer loved her, nor she him and yet, the child was his. All manner of fearful thoughts rushed through her mind. What to tell John, what to tell Billy! When to tell anybody!

She stared at herself in the mirror. "Now, Mary Dawson, calm yourself, you're married and your husband is the father of this child." She repeated the affirmation to herself several times as she gathered up Nancy and ran downstairs to Annie's single end.

Annie hurried to the door in response to the frantic knocking.

"Mary," she exclaimed. "What on earth is wrong?"

Mary rushed past her into the kitchen and plonked Nancy on the floor. Pacing up and down the small space she finally turned and faced Annie.

"I'm pregnant," she announced.

Annie stared at her in disbelief. "Pregnant?"

Mary bit her lip. "To Billy," she added abruptly.

Annie felt a mixture of anger and pity boil inside her. "Oh, Mary, how *could you*, how *could you*!" and she too began pacing the floor.

Mary burst into tears. "I didn't want to be pregnant and anyway, it's all your fault, it was the night you disappeared and Billy got drunk and…"

"Stop it," shouted Annie, taking Mary by the shoulders and shaking her. "It's no one's fault, no one's to blame, it just happened."

Mary crumpled into the chair and picked up Nancy, who was beginning to sense her mother's distress. "It's alright," she assured her, burying her face into the child's neck.

"Does Billy know?" asked Annie, trying to calm her own nerves.

Mary shook her head. "No, but he's bound to know sooner or later."

"If it's his, then it's alright, isn't it?" reasoned Annie. "You'll just have to give up John Anderson and make a life for yourself and your children as best you can."

Mary looked at her sister with pleading eyes. "Don't ask me to give up John," she begged. "Not that."

Annie's heart went out to her young sister. "Mary," she cooed softly to her. "There's nothing else to do. You must think of Nancy and your child to be. What will happen to them if you leave?"

Mary drew a deep breath. "I could get rid of it," she stated unemotionally.

Annie drew back in horror, remembering her own pregnancy and delivery. She shook her head from side to side. "No, Mary, *no*, you can't do that, not that."

Mary's petulance reared up. "And why *not*, Annie Pepper? I don't want to have Billy's child. I didn't want to have the first one." She picked up Nancy. "I don't care if you help me or not," she added bravely. "But I'm not having his child."

Annie caught her by both shoulders. "Alright," she nodded. "I'll help, just don't do anything foolish till I speak with Jessie."

"Oh Annie," Mary began, weeping again. "Jessie, mustn't know. Please, say you won't tell her.

Annie held her sister close and smoothed her hair. "It's alright," she told her. "It's alright." But Annie knew it wasn't and she also knew that now she'd agreed to help, Mary would hold her to it.

Annie knocked on at her looms the following day and braced herself for the din of the machinery to fill her head. She'd never got used to the noise and always tensed at the racket.

Billy watched her out of the corner of his eye and waited.

At dinner-time the mill whistle sounded and the weavers moved, as one, to the door. But Billy had anticipated Annie's departure and caught her arm as she turned to join the others.

She could feel the pressure of his fingers tightening in measure with his voice.

"Can I visit you?" he breathed. "Soon?"

Annie's jaw clenched as she pulled her arm free. "I'm not open to callers, Mr Dawson," she responded defensively. "And, in particular, I'm not open to you."

Billy nodded, his eyes narrowed with hurt. "Alright, Annie, but remember, I can wait."

Annie felt a wave of anger towards him wash over her. "Then wait, Billy," she replied, her voice trembling. "Just like I waited for you."

Billy's grip tightened even further on her arm again. "Annie," he pleaded with her. "She was with child, my child - I had to marry her."

Annie almost blurted out about their son, but stopped herself. "Stay away from me Billy," she warned him. "Just *stay away.*"

She pulled herself free and ran the full length of the weaving flat to the door.

Jessie was waiting for her at the top of the metal stair and stopped her flight. "Annie, Annie," she called. "What's wrong lassie, you're going to hurt yourself rushing round like that."

"Help me, Jessie," she begged. "Help me."

Jessie folded her arm around her shoulders and led her down stairs and outside. "Whatever it is, Annie, it can be fixed, just remember that."

Annie sniffed and nodded, her emotions getting the better of her.

Jessie was her only friend, and it was Jessie she turned to, yet again, despite her promise to Mary not to tell her.

"Will you come and see me tonight Jessie, please."

Jessie nodded. "I'll come," she replied. "But you must tell me what's bothering you, or I can't do anything to help."

Annie nodded in agreement. "I must talk to someone, Jessie, and I want it to be you."

That night, Jessie knocked at Annie's door, not knowing what to expect but not expecting what Annie eventually told her. She omitted to mention John Anderson, Mary and Billy's baby, or anything that had gone before, but asked instead if Jessie knew an abortionist as she, Annie, was pregnant with Joe's child.

Jessie eyed her with suspicion on hearing the news. "Joe Cassiday may be a bit of a lad," she told Annie. "But fathering a bairn out o' wedlock doesn't sound like Joe."

Annie felt guilt well up in her as she compounded the lie. "Please, Jessie, just believe me. I need to get rid of it. Joe and me have parted and I can't have the baby on my own."

"Alright, lassie," she soothed Annie. "I know a woman who'll help.

Calm down."

Jessie gave Annie the name. "Lily Cooke," she whispered, almost convinced that someone was listening to their conversation. "She lives up in the Hilltown, used to be a nurse at the infirmary. She'll fix it for you."

Annie clasped her hand. "Thank you, Jessie, thank you."

"But mind, it'll cost money. A woman like her doesn't come cheap."

"I know," Annie assured her. "My sister will give me the money."

"And as for that Joe Cassiday," Jessie fumed. "Somebody should tell 'im what he's done to you."

Annie grabbed her shoulders. "*No*, Jessie, promise me you won't say anything to Joe."

"Alright, alright," Jessie responded quickly, shocked at Annie's vehemence.

"If that's what you want!"

Annie nodded vigorously. "It is, Jessie, it is."

Jessie left soon after nine. Annie leant against the closed door and breathed a huge sigh of relief. Jessie had come to her rescue again. She would never be able to repay all her kindness and she hated having to lie to her, but there had been no choice. She'd see Mary on Sunday at the hall and tell her where to find Lily Cooke. The rest would be up to her. Lying seemed to be becoming a way of life for her and she didn't like it. Secrets and lies seemed to fill her days.

She stretched her arms above her head and rubbed her neck and shoulders. She was tired, tired of it all and weary with the burden she was now carrying.

She pulled off her heavy boots and wriggled her toes. The action took her back to the stream that day with Billy and she could almost feel the cool water running over her legs. Her eyes closed and pictures of Billy flooded into her imagination. Her breathing became laboured and soon she was shaking with sorrow. She had loved him so much and would have laid down her life for him, but he had chosen Mary and now, she was pregnant with his second child and he didn't even know. Nor would he know, if Mary went ahead with her plan.

At first she had been so lost in her thoughts she hadn't heard the faint knocking at the window, but when she did, a cold fear gripped her.

"Who's there?" she called trying to keep the panic out of her voice. The tapping began again. "Who's there I say?" she called louder. The tapping ceased.

Billy's voice answered. "Open the door, Annie," he said, his voice low and pleading. "I've a letter for you."

Annie's heart was pounding. "Put it through the door, Billy," she ordered. "I'm not letting you in."

She heard the whisper of paper being pushed under the door and then silence.

Cautiously she lifted the candle and crept to the door. A small, pale envelope lay on the floor. She picked it up and held it to the light. It was addressed to her in the familiar writing of Bella. Annie breathed a sigh of relief and returned to the small kitchen to read its contents.

'Dear Annie,' it began, 'I am well and happy and Dr Adams and the Missus are very good to me. Cook says I'll make a fine parlour maid if I'm good and do as I'm told and sometimes she lets me go to the market with her to shop for the vegetables. It's grand there, Annie, all green and lovely smells.

'We had a scare with Master Adams the other week - he's walking now and fell into the pond in the garden. Nearly drowned he did. But the Doctor saved him in time and Mother Superior from the Poor House came and comforted the Missus.

'He's a real handsome lad, Annie, all dark hair and eyes. He'll turn a few heads when he's older that one.

'I hope you're well. Do write and tell me how you are. I miss you very much. Bella.'

Annie hugged the letter to her. 'Little Bella,' she thought. 'How brave she is. She had no one in the world to turn to and had so much love to give.'

She would write to her the very next night and tell her where she was now living. She didn't want any more excuses for Billy to call.

Annie didn't sleep well that night. Nightmare visions of the child in the letter, face down in the pond, kept disturbing her rest.

Joe Cassiday was slumped in a chair, gazing into the flames of the glowing coals as they burned in the grate.

"You alright, Joe?" asked Charlie quietly. "You've not said much since that encounter you had with Billy Dawson."

Joe lit another cigarette and inhaled deeply. "Nothing to tell," he stated bluntly.

"And Annie," Charlie prodded. "How's your Annie?"

"She's not *my* Annie," Joe erupted suddenly. "Don't call her *my* Annie, Charlie."

As quickly as his temper had flared, it died again, but was replaced by a deep sobbing that wracked his body.

"Joe, Joe, what is it?" Charlie was really concerned now - he'd never seen Joe so upset. Not Joe, with his ready grin and cheery word for everyone.

Joe held his head in his hands and pushed his fingers through his hair again and again. Charlie waited till the worst of the pain had passed and Joe finally raised his eyes to look at him.

"You were right Charlie."

"What about?"

"You said low morals ran in families and you were right."

"Are you meaning Annie?" Charlie asked, already sensing the answer.

Joe lit another cigarette and nodded.

"She's not a virgin Charlie. She's been with another man before me."

His eyes and voice were bleak with hurt and disillusionment.

"Billy Dawson?" Charlie asked simply. Joe nodded.

"When?"

Joe blew rings of smoke in the air. "A while ago, in Ireland. Says she fell in love with him." Joe felt the hurt rising again and held his breath to try to stop the process. "Just like she fell in love with me…" The sobbing began again.

"Women," Charlie muttered. "Better off without them, Joe - bring nothing but sorrow."

Joe nodded in agreement. "Thing is Charlie," he said, lost in his hopelessness, "I loved her."

Knowing there was nothing to do to ease Joe's pain, Charlie remained silent.

The heaving of Joe's chest gradually eased, till he was perfectly still. He sat in the gathering darkness, only the occasional blinking of his eyes signalling he was still alive. The clock on the mantelpiece chimed out the quarters and the hours till it struck midnight.

"I have to get out of this place," Joe announced quietly.

"You're free to leave anytime, Joe," replied Charlie, who'd watched with him through the pain. "There's no lock on this door."

"Not from here Charlie," Joe added tonelessly. "From Dundee."

Charlie nodded. "And where would you go Joe?" he asked gently. "Back to the old country maybe?"

"No," Joe answered. "Not back there. I don't know as yet, but I'm going somewhere." He rose from his chair, his body drained of all emotion.

"And what about Annie?" reminded Charlie. "Is she really out of your life?"

Charlie clenched his teeth and nodded. "There's no way back to that one, Charlie, any woman who gives herself to a man before wedlock has no place with me."

"Even if that man were yourself?"

Joe locked his eyes on Charlie's. "But he wasn't was he?" he said bitterly. "He wasn't."

Charlie knew it was pointless to speak further that night. "Goodnight Joe," he said, as the tall figure of his brother passed him.

Joe's hand brushed his shoulder. "Goodnight."

"Joe went through the motions of living over the next few weeks, while Charlie watched and waited for signs of his recovery. "Just remember, I'm always here for you, no matter what," he said one night, dishing up the potato soup he'd made for their supper. Joe felt tears welling in his eyes again and hugged Charlie to prevent him from seeing them.

"I know," he murmured. "I know." The two men ate the hot soup in silence, dipping chunks of bread into it to bulk up its thinness.

"Why don't you go down the Thrums for a drink later," Charlie suggested, not for the first time, but this time, he got a response.

Joe sniffed and inhaled the warmth of the kitchen. "I might do," he told Charlie.

"There's nothing like a pint or two of ale to put the world to rights," Charlie added, sensing a breakthrough.

Joe blinked at his brother, conscious of his concern.

"Enjoy your life Joe," Charlie added earnestly. "It's too short for this pain you're in."

Charlie was right and Joe knew it. Nothing was going to undo what had happened.

"Will you join me there, later on?" he asked, taking in a deep breath.

Charlie nodded, smiling with relief. "When I've done a few things here," he said.

"You can fuss like an old woman sometimes, Charlie," Joe said softly. "But I'm glad you're me brother."

Joe pulled on his jacket and angled his bonnet over one eye. "I'll see you later then," he called over his shoulder, as the darkness of the night swallowed him up. He made his way down the narrow lane and as he turned into King Street where the lights of the Thurms Bar glowed in the distance, a hand tapped him on the shoulder. Joe turned to face the form of a soldier.

"Is there anywhere a bloke can get a drink around here?" he asked Joe politely.

Joe looked at him from top to toe.

The soldier was a fine figure of a man in black doublet and tartan kilt, and a smile of admiration flickered at Joe's mouth. "I'm looking for a drink myself," he replied. "And the pub's within spitting distance."

The soldier acknowledged the statement with a slight incline of his head.

"You can join me in a pint of ale, if you like," Joe said.

The soldier fell in line with his steps and together they entered the hubbub of the bar.

"And what regiment are you?" asked Joe, ordering two pints as he admired the handsome uniform.

"Black Watch."

"Black Watch," Joe repeated to himself, a wistfulness stirring in his soul. He handed the soldier his glass of beer. "Well, here's to you, soldier man," he said, as they clinked their glasses.

As they drank, the wistfulness quickly became restlessness and then a need to know in Joe's soul.

"So, what's it like in the Black Watch?" he asked. "I mean, really like?"

Joe listened, becoming more and more enraptured as the soldier told his tales of bravery and camaraderie. This was the way out for him he'd been looking for, he told himself, unable to understand why he hadn't thought of it before. He'd join the forces and, in particular, the Black Watch.

Instead of going to the docks the next day, Joe went to the recruiting office and, standing smartly to attention, asked the Recruitment Sergeant if he could sign up.

The Sergeant was a fearsome sight and for a minute Joe's resolve weakened. Black whiskers glistened under his nose and steely blue eyes fixed their unblinking gaze on him.

"Name?" the Sergeant asked smartly, coming over to Joe and pacing around him like a panther waiting to pounce.

"Cassiday," replied Joe, equally smartly. The end of Sergeant McKay's measuring stick flicked around Joe's hairline before pointing to his boots. Joe glanced down in dismay at the dull footwear.

"Eyes front," rasped the military voice.

The Sergeant made his way back to a desk and sat down, motioning Joe to come closer.

"The Black Watch is the finest regiment in the world, son," he intoned in a husky whisper. "Do you understand, *theeee finest.*"

Joe nodded quickly.

"And, we only take the *creeeeam* of the crop."

Joe nodded again.

"So, what would we be wanting with an Irish Paddy like yourself?"

Joe felt himself flinch at the insult. "I may be an Irish Paddy," he returned. "But I'm *theeee finest* Irish Paddy in Dundee."

The Sergeant's face broke into a huge grin and, throwing back his head, he began to laugh from his belly.

"You'll do," he told Joe. "I like a man who's proud, just like the Black Watch."

Joe relaxed.

"So, I can join then?" he asked.

Sergeant McKay dipped a pen in the ink bottle on the desk and offered it to Joe.

"Sign here, Cassiday," he instructed. "And welcome to the Black Watch."

"I report for the medical examination on the first of September," he told an anxious Charlie. "And I can't wait."

Charlie looked at his younger brother. "Are you sure you're joining for the right reasons, Joe?"

Joe swung round to face him. "I'm joining 'cause that's what I want to do, Charlie, no other reason."

By the look on Joe's face, Charlie knew not to question him further. "I'll miss you," he said instead.

"And I you, big brother, but some things just have to be."

It was Jessie who told Annie the news.

"Joined the Black Watch," she said. "Fancy that. I can just picture him in his uniform," mused Jessie. "Kilt and all." Jessie became aware of Annie's silence. "Oh, I'm sorry lassie," she comforted. "I forgot for a minute what he did to you."

Annie forced a smile. "Well, that's all in the past, Jessie, and there's no going back now."

Jessie eyed her quizzically. "I have to admit, Annie, you're very calm about everything considering your planning to get rid o' his bairn."

Annie pulled herself up sharply.

"Have you been to see Mrs Cook yet?" Jessie queried.

Annie felt herself colour. "Yes," she stammered. "I went last night… it's all arranged."

"Is it now," Jessie replied, anxiously. "Are you sure it's what you want to do, Annie?"

Annie felt hotter. "I'm sure," she replied. "Now stop asking me all these questions Jessie. Let's get back to work, or we'll be late."

Jessie followed her back to their looms, more worried than ever. Something didn't seem right but it wasn't like Annie to lie, but Jessie had to accept she knew what she was doing.

Billy's figure loomed over Annie as she knocked on. "Did you get your letter?" he asked.

Annie's arm moved towards the wooden lever, continuing to start her loom as through she had'nt heard him.

He caught her hand. "I asked you if you got your letter alright?"

Annie nodded.

"Who was it from?" he asked, still gripping her wrist.

"No one you know," replied Annie, wincing with the tightness of his grip.

Their eyes locked for what seemed like a lifetime before Billy released her.

"Let me see you," he asked, his voice suddenly softening. "Just for a while?"

A thousand thoughts flashed through her head in a few seconds. Billy pulling the flax, Billy holding her, Billy loving her then Billy leaving her and marrying Mary and her resolve hardened again.

"I've nothing to say to you, Billy Dawson," she replied to his request. "Now let me get on with my work."

Billy turned on his heel and marched quickly back down the weaving flat to his desk.

His heart was pounding with the exchange. It seemed the more Annie rejected his advances the more urgent they became to him.

Jessie did not miss the exchange of words that took place between them and, although she could not hear what was said, their expressions spoke louder than words.

That evening, Mary was waiting for her to return from the mill. Her face was whiter than normal as she rocked the sleeping Nancy in her arms.

"I need to speak to you urgently, Annie, before Billy comes home."

Annie acknowledged her anxiety and hurried along the close to her door.

She took Nancy from her and placed the child on her bed, covering her lightly with a wool blanket, before turning to Mary.

"Tell me," she urged.

Mary's eyes were filled with fear. "I've been to see Mrs Cook," she told Annie. "And I've to go back… to have it done… on Friday night."

Annie looked at her sister. "Are you sure you want to go ahead with this,

Mary?"

"I'm so frightened, Annie, Mrs Cook's a horrible woman. All she wanted to know was did I have the money and she's got this dreadful black cat…" Mary began to shake.

"C'mon, now, c'mon," comforted Annie, her heart going out to her sister. "It'll be alright."

Mary began to sob uncontrollably, "Please come with me, Annie," she begged between great gulps of air. "I can't go alone, I just can't."

Annie held her tightly. "It's alright, I'll come with you, it's alright."

It was only the stirring of Nancy which forced Mary to try to fight back the waves of tears which kept surging through her.

"Nancy's wakening," said Annie. "Dry your eyes now or Billy's going to be asking what's wrong. I'll wait for you at the top of the lane steps on Friday." She passed Nancy over and gave Mary a last reassuring hug. "It'll be alright, Mary, I'll see you on Friday."

Mary disappeared through the door and left Annie trembling at the prospect of what was to come. She knew the pain of childbirth but nothing of abortion and her ignorance fuelled even more fears as to what Mrs Cook would do to Mary.

CHAPTER 12

A cold wind was gusting up Victoria Road adding to the chill Annie already felt. She pulled her wool shawl tightly round her shoulders, as Mary's small frame ascended the steps towards her. Annie put her arm around her.

"It'll soon be over," she whispered. "Remember I'll be with you all the time." Mary nodded, her whole body shaking.

They crossed Victoria Road and walked towards the Hilltown, their heads down and faces set in grim lines.

"Mary!" a voice called, "Mary, *wait.*" Footsteps hurried up behind them. "Aren't you coming to the hall?" Isabella Anderson caught up with them. Mary pulled her shawl over her head leaving Annie to answer.

"Mary's not very well, Mrs Anderson," she explained lamely. "I'm just taking her to the Doctor's."

Isabella Anderson immediately looked concerned and moved towards Mary. "Is there anything I can do?" she asked trying to get a look at her.

"No," interceded Annie, quickly. "Nothing. She'll be fine, thank you for your concern. Now if you'll excuse us, we're late already."

Annie put her arm round Mary protectively and hurried her away.

Isabella Anderson stood looking after them till they disappeared from sight.

"What are you looking at?" asked her husband, joining her. "The hall's this way," he reminded her, turning her round to face the other way.

"I've just seen Mary Dawson and her sister, Annie."

John Anderson stood very still.

"Annie says she's taking Mary to the doctor, but..."

"But?" asked John.

Isabella shrugged her shoulders. "It's probably something and nothing John, she just seemed to be acting very strangely, that's all."

"Annie or Mary?" he asked.

"Why, both of them, really, but Mary in particular. It was as though she was afraid to speak to me."

John Anderson's mind sought for an explanation to give his wife. "I'm sure you've got it wrong, Isabella, Mary's your friend. Anyway, I'm sure you'll see her again sooner or later and you can reassure yourself everything's fine. Now, the service can't start without you and your Songsters, so..." John indicated the door of the hall.

Isabella seemed to relax. "You're probably right, John." But nonetheless, her instincts told her something was wrong with Mary, very wrong.

Mrs Cook's house was situated up a narrow pend off the Hilltown. A gas mantle spluttered at its entrance and seemed to add to the unease already well-established in Annie's mind.

She knocked at the brown door, splashed with rain and grime. It creaked open revealing the wrinkled face of its owner.

"Mrs Cook?" asked Annie. The woman nodded. "My sister's come to see you."

The crone squinted into the gloom and, on recognising Mary, indicated they should follow her.

The kitchen smelled overwhelmingly of cats. Annie caught her breath and held Mary's hand tighter.

"Have you got the money?" she asked, never meeting their eyes, but holding out her hand.

Mary dug into the pocket of her skirt and brought out a small brown envelope. "It's what you asked," she ventured feebly.

Mrs Cook sniffed and pushed the envelope into her apron pocket. "That way then," she pointed to a door at the back of the kitchen. "Take off your bloomers and lie on the bed, I'll be through directly."

Mary thought she was going to faint as she tried to propel her legs forward towards the door. The smell of cats filled her nostrils and the terror of entering into that other room brought on a bout of nausea.

"I'm going to be sick," she murmured to Annie, leaning heavily on her for support. Annie began to panic as the whole situation became surreal.

"Mary, you can't go through with this, please, God knows what she'll do to you in there."

Mrs Cook waited while Mary tried to steady herself. "You've paid the price, lassie, might as well get your money's worth," she stated, unmoved by Mary's plight.

Mary began to walk towards the door again. "I have to, Annie," she whispered. "I have to."

Annie covered her face with her hands, unable to watch her sister anymore. She heard the door close, leaving her alone in the kitchen. Her heart was pounding in her breast and she had to fight back the urge to run as fast and as far away from this awful place as she could.

Mary's scream pierced her head and her blood ran cold.

"My God, she's done it," she whispered to herself. "Oh! Mary, God help you."

Annie clenched her hands into fists to try to stop them trembling as the door of the room opened.

Mary came out followed by Mrs Cook. "Take her home now," she told Annie. "And make sure the blood flows." Mary's face was chalk-white as Annie rushed to her side.

"Mary, Mary," she murmured through tears of anger and fear. "It's over now, it's over now."

Mary nodded and clung to Annie. "Don't ever tell Billy," she pleaded, her voice weak with shock.

Annie nodded assuringly. "I won't Mary, don't worry." But Billy had to be told something. Mary was in such a state, even he was bound to notice.

Slowly they made their way back to William Lane, Mary breathing in the night air in an effort to restore some life to her body and calm her soul.

"Please come with me," she asked Annie. "Speak to Billy, make it alright."

Annie nodded. "Don't worry, I'll not let you face him alone."

She wasn't sure how she was going to deal with Billy, but she couldn't desert Mary, not now, not ever.

Billy was sleeping off a Friday night's ale when they got home, his feet propped against the mantelpiece and his head lolling on to his chest.

Mary winced as a pain circled her womb. "Get me to the bed," she whispered to Annie. "I'll be alright once I'm lying down."

Carefully, Annie manoeuvred her past Billy and onto the bed. Mary flopped down like a rag doll.

"Try to sleep," Annie told her. "I'll come back tomorrow morning after Billy's gone to the mill.

Mary nodded feebly. "Thanks Annie," she moaned. "Thanks…"

Annie straightened up and crept from the room, thanking God she didn't have to explain Mary's distress to Billy that night. "Tomorrow, would be better," she told herself, but tomorrow was worse.

The loud banging on her window brought Annie sharply awake. "What is it?" she called, rushing to climb out of bed as she pulled her shawl over her nightgown.

"It's Mary," came Billy's voice high with anxiety. "Come quick, she's bleeding to death."

Mary felt the adrenaline surge through her body. She threw open the door.

Billy's face was ashen. "I don't know what's wrong with her Annie, but she wants you to come *now*."

Annie pushed past him and dashed up the winding stairwell, her feet barely touching the steps.

Mary looked paler than before, if that was possible.

"Mary?" Annie called her name. "It's Annie, everything's going to be alright, I'll get the doctor."

Mary's eyes were closed and her breathing was shallow.

"Fetch the Doctor, Billy, *quickly*."

Billy nodded and was gone.

Annie could do nothing. Clots of blood were on the floor where Mary had tried to get up, but now her strength was almost gone and her face lay lifeless on the pillow.

"Don't let Mary die, God," Annie prayed, trying to keep a grip on her emotions. "Please."

The Doctor followed Billy into the kitchen.

"How long has she been like this?" he asked Annie. Annie looked at Billy.

"I just woke up and she was lying there, moaning… I don't know how long for."

"About four hours," Annie estimated.

The Doctor swiftly took her blood pressure.

He looked at Annie, trying to ascertain her presence of mind.

"She's lost a lot of blood," he said bluntly. "She'll be dead before morning if she doesn't stop haemorrhaging."

Annie felt faint.

"How did it happen?" the doctor asked.

Annie knew she had to tell the truth. "She's had an abortion, Doctor," she replied.

The doctor clenched his teeth.

"You mean she's been butchered."

Annie felt sick. "Help her, Doctor," she begged. "Don't let her die."

"I'm afraid it's out of my hands," he replied. "It's up to God now, all we can do is pray. I'll call back in the morning."

The doctor left Annie alone and went outside with Billy.

On his return, Billy knelt beside her at Mary's side. "Why, Annie?" he asked. "Why did she want to get rid of the baby?"

Annie felt only fear for her sister's life. "Because you don't love her anymore," she told him. "Because she fears you, because she's Mary…" Annie tailed off, words seeming pointless.

Mary stirred and opened her eyes. "Annie," she smiled weakly. "You're here."

Annie held her hand. "Yes Mary, I'm here."

"Where's Billy?" she asked.

"I'm here Mary," he replied moving closer to her. "The Doctor says you'll be fine."

"So tired…" she replied drifting into unconsciousness.

Annie sat with her sister all night. The Doctor arrived the following morning, his features set in a grim expression.

He sounded Mary's chest and took her blood pressure again.

"She's still with us," he told Annie and Billy. "But she's lost a lot of blood."

"Is she past the worst?" asked Annie, willing the Doctor to say 'yes'.

"No, lassie," he replied. "She's not past the worst and by rights, she should be dead."

Annie jumped to her feet. "She's *not* going to die, do you hear me, she's going to *live*."

The Doctor too, rose to his feet. "I hope you're right, Missie, I hope you're right.

He left Annie with a draft for the blood loss and instructions that she must get Mary to take some sustenance.

Annie ordered Billy to make some sweet tea.

"Mary," she called softly. "Waken up Mary, and drink your tea."

Mary's eyes flickered as Annie lifted her head to the spoonful of warm liquid.

"Just a little," she coaxed. Mary felt the sweetness touch her tongue and swallowed.

"Good girl," encouraged Annie, filling the spoon again. "Now, just a little more."

Billy watched in silence as Annie carefully spooned tiny amounts of liquid down Mary's throat, all the time encouraging her to drink a little more.

"Will she be alright?" he asked, once the tea had been drunk.

Annie returned Mary's head to the pillow. "I don't know Billy," she replied, looking at his worried face. "I just don't know."

For seven days, Annie barely left Mary's side. Billy looked after Nancy and fetched and carried on Annie's instructions. On the third day, Mary regained a tinge of colour as the beef tea and sweetened milk began to work their way into her bloodstream, nourishing and replenishing the loss and by day five she was beginning to take solids. The Doctor came in every day until he was sure Mary was on the mend.

He shook Annie's hand. "She's had a fine nurse in you, Miss Pepper, it's just a pity it happened in the first place." He squeezed her hand kindly. "Get her to come in and see me at the surgery when she's on her feet."

By the tenth day, Mary felt strong enough to test her legs and promptly fainted.

"You're trying to do things too fast," Annie chided her, once she had regained consciousness. "Just sit for a while, with your legs over the side of the bed and let your body catch up with you." But Annie was smiling as she said it; Mary was going to be alright.

Billy had watched in awe of Annie's strength and perseverance and when she announced she was returning to her own place, he did nothing to try to stop her.

"She owes you her life, Annie," he told her. "And I owe you my thanks and deepest respect."

Annie acknowledged the compliment. "Just make sure she continues to get better, Billy, she's my only sister and I love her dearly."

Billy hung his head. "I'll make sure."

John Anderson was beside himself with worry. He hadn't seen nor heard anything of Mary for four weeks. She hadn't attended any of the services and this, coupled with Isabella's speculations about something being wrong with her, had done nothing to allay his fears.

"Are you alright, John?" asked his wife, watching the frown on his face deepen into lines of worry.

He looked up. "Yes," he answered quickly. "Why do you ask?"

Isabella shook her head and returned to her embroidery. "Oh, nothing, you just looked… preoccupied."

"I suppose I am a bit worried," John continued, taking the opportunity to bring Mary's name into the conversation. "I was just thinking we hadn't seen Mary Dawson for a while and after that encounter you had with her and her sister, well… I was just wondering if she was alright!"

Isabella put down her needle. "Do you think I should visit her, see how she is?"

John let his shoulders relax. "I think that's an excellent idea Isabella, and soon, I wouldn't like her to think we've forgotten her."

"I'm sure she doesn't think any such thing," she reassured him. "I'll go tomorrow evening."

Mary was sitting quietly reading when Isabella called. She rose slowly and went to the door.

A smile spread across Isabella's face. "Why Mary," she said holding out both her hands in greeting. "I'm so pleased to see you. John and I have been quite worried about you."

Mary invited her in and returned to her chair.

Isabella watched the slowness of her movements and became concerned. "Is something wrong, Mary? You seem tired."

Mary shook her head. "Nothing's wrong, Isabella, but I have been quite ill these last few weeks and it'll be another while yet before I'm fully able to resume my duties at the Hall."

Isabella pulled her chair closer. "Oh, Mary, I'm not here about your duties at the Hall, I'm here because we were concerned at not seeing you and, we were right to be so, it would seem."

"My sister's been looking after me just fine, but thank you for coming."

Isabella stood up. "I can see you're not fully recovered yet, Mary," she said quietly. "So I'll leave you in peace." She moved towards the door. "Don't get up, I'll see myself out," she called over her shoulder. "By the way," she turned to face Mary. "What illness did you have? I hope it wasn't too serious."

Mary hesitated for a moment considering her answer. "Oh, just women's trouble, you know Isabella," she told her. "The price we pay for being female."

Isabella wasn't sure exactly what Mary meant by 'women's trouble' but thought it best not to ask further. "I'll tell John you're fine then, shall I?"

Mary nodded. "Yes Isabella, tell him I'm fine."

After she had gone, Mary sat for a long time, staring at the coals burning in their iron basket. She had almost lost her life for the love of John Anderson and the fear of Billy, yet none of them had been there for her in her time of need. But Annie had. She owed Annie her life and she knew it.

A wave of love and thanks washed over her, wiping out the pain of their past differences.

"I'll repay you a thousand-fold Annie," she vowed silently, "if it's the last thing I do."

Billy's form moved past the window and opened the door into the kitchen.

He had never said anything about the abortion and why she had done what she'd done but he had stopped drinking at nights and spent all his time looking after Nancy and working at the mill. He still slept in the other room, but Mary was glad of it, especially now.

"Was that Isabella Anderson I just passed in the close?" Billy asked.

"It was."

"What did she want then, to bring Jesus to you, or just to pry?" Billy couldn't keep the sarcasm out of his voice.

"Neither, Billy," Mary countered. "Just to see how I was."

Billy began filling the scuttle with coal from the bunker. "Time you stopped all that nonsense anyway, singing hymns and banging tambourines. Your place is at home with Nancy, looking after the house instead of mixing with all those Holy Joes."

Mary felt a shimmer of anxiety, as she heard the beginnings of impatience in Billy's voice. "You're probably right, Billy," she placated him, not feeling strong enough to argue.

"Then you'll stop going?" he asked her.

Mary flinched. He'd backed her into a corner from which she could see no way out. "If you forbid me to go, Billy, then as my husband, I must obey your wishes."

Billy nodded. "Then I forbid you."

He picked up Nancy and took her through to the other room leaving Mary alone in the kitchen.

She could feel the heat of the fire pressing against her and went to the door to breathe in the outside air. She was weary of Billy telling her what she could and couldn't do and helpless to do anything but accept her situation.

She looked up into the twilight, her eyes glistening with tears. "It wasn't meant to be like this," she told the emptiness. "Maybe it would have been better if I'd died."

Annie returned to her work and was immediately met by Jessie.

"Annie," she called to her. "I've been so worried about you."

Annie nodded. "I'm alright Jessie," she assured her. "It's all over. Now I just want to get back to normal and get on with my work."

Jessie understood but not without a parting shot about Joe. "That Joe Cassiday needn't show his face around here again," she confirmed to Annie. "Not after what he's done."

"Please Jessie, let's just forget about it. It's past now, let it go."

Jessie's lips formed a thin line. "You're a brave woman Annie Pepper," she said stoutly. "And I'll respect your wishes."

Annie smiled. "Thanks Jessie," she said. "For everything."

"There's Mister Dawson, at last," pointed out Jessie. "He's been away from his work for a while, but nobody knows why. I don't suppose you…?"

"No Jessie," Annie replied firmly. "I don't know why, and I don't want to."

"I'll see you at dinner-time then."

Annie nodded. Her looms leapt into life and her expert eyes watched as the shuttle sped across the warp. "At last," she breathed. "Things are beginning to feel normal."

Joe Cassiday marched up King Street in his new uniform. The Black Watch tartan kilt swung rhythmically as he walked and his bonnet was set at a jaunty angle. No one could have felt prouder of the uniform. He'd been through the rigours of base camp and was fit and full of energy and every eye, both male and female, watched him walk by.

"Hey, Joe!" called out one of his old drinking buddies, grinning from ear to ear. "Where's your breeks?"

Joe bowed and feigned surprise to find he was trouserless. "Buy me a pint of ale tonight, and I'll tell you," he laughed.

His brother was waiting for him at the end of Todburn Lane and saw him swing proudly up William Lane. The two brothers hugged each other, to the cheers of a crowd of children who'd followed Joe from Cowgate School. Joe tossed a handful of coppers into the air and there was a wild scramble to retrieve the coins.

"I've got two," shouted one of the urchins.

"I've got three," boasted another, only to have them pinched from his hand by a bigger sibling.

The youngsters dispersed, running pell-mell to the sweetie shop to spend their coins.

"You're looking well, Joe," Charlie stated.

Joe nodded. "I feel well, Charlie. Joining the Black Watch is the best thing I've ever done."

They made their way along Todburn Lane to their small home.

"You'll not have heard, of course, will you?"

Joe looked at his brother. "Heard what?"

"That girl of yours, Annie Pepper."

Joe dumped his kitbag and turned towards Charlie. "What about Annie Pepper," he asked, suddenly feeling tense.

"The talk is she was pregnant to you and had the bairn got rid of when you left her."

Joe couldn't believe his ears. "Who's saying this, Charlie?" he asked coldly, anger beginning to build in his muscles.

"Oh, you know, nobody and everybody."

"I never bedded her Charlie, if she was with child, it wasn't mine."

Charlie shrugged. "I just thought you should know what's being said before you got it from someone else."

"Is she alright?" Joe asked quietly.

"She must be, she's back working at Baxters I'm told."

If Joe had thought he had got Annie out of his system, he was wrong. All the feelings of tenderness and love he had fought to banish from his heart, rushed to the surface.

"I'll see you later, Charlie," Joe announced standing up and replacing his hat. "There's someone I have to see."

"Don't do anything foolish now, Joseph Cassiday," Charlie called after him.

But the door had slammed and Joe had gone.

He was waiting for Annie on her return from the mill.

At first, she didn't recognise the soldier but as she got closer she realised it was Joe and her heart leapt. But it soon fell again when she saw the expression on his face. Annie braced herself for the confrontation.

"Hello Annie," he said, inclining his head and doffing his hat.

"Hello Joe."

Annie turned the key in her lock as he spoke again. "How are you?"

"Fine," she answered, opening the door. "Are you coming in, then, or do you want the whole land to hear what you've to say?"

Joe followed her in. "What makes you think I've something to say?" he asked.

Annie met his gaze. "Judging by the expression on your face, Joe

Cassiday, I'd say you have a lot you want to say."

"Charlie tells me…"he began.

Annie swiftly interrupted his revelations. "oh, I see, *Charlie* told you. And what *has* Charlie told you? Gossip and lies no doubt."

Joe felt his anger rumbling beneath the surface. "Is it gossip and lies that you've had an abortion Annie, and that you've been telling everyone the bairn's mine?"

Annie felt as if she'd been hit with a sledgehammer. "I think you'd better go, Joe," she told him, her voice ice-cold and her heart wounded. "If that's what you think, then so be it."

Joe looked up to the heavens. "I *know* it wasn't mine, because we never slept together, and it doesn't take a great stretch of the imagination to know who's bairn it was, but all I want to know is…"

"*Get out*," Annie screamed at him. And take your filthy mind with you."

Joe felt sick. This wasn't what he had meant to happen. "Annie," he began. "I'm sorry… sorry for everything. Help me to understand!"

Annie sensed his sincerity and calmed down. "I can't tell you any more than this. I haven't been pregnant, not to you or anyone, and I haven't had an abortion."

Joe stared at her in confusion. "Then, who has…?"

Annie held up her hand to his lips. "Please," she begged. "Don't ask me anymore because I can't tell you. Now, go," she urged him, feeling herself being drawn to him again. "Your brother will be waiting for you."

The comment stung Joe's pride. "Alright," he answered. "I won't stay where I'm not welcome, but if you want anything, Annie," he told her. "Just ask."

Annie bit her lip. She wanted everything from Joe - love, security, children.

"I will," she replied, pulling her shoulders back and lengthening her neck. "Now, I'll be saying goodnight."

Joe nodded and pulled his cap over his wavy hair. "Goodbye Annie."

"Good bye Joe."

CHAPTER 13

As Mary's physical strength returned, her emotional strength diminished. More and more, she stayed indoors, singing softly to Nancy and polishing and polishing, virtually anything that took a shine.

If Billy noticed her unhappiness, he never commented, his routine now revolved round his time at the mill and Nancy. He spoke little and when he did, it was with the minimum of words and only to speak of their daughter. For three months Mary stood the silence and isolation till she could stand it no longer.

"Will you *never* forgive me?" she wailed in desperation at the end of another silent evening.

Billy folded his paper and rose from his chair. "I've nothing to say to you my dear, let alone forgive you for. Now, I think it's time I went to bed.

Mary sprang up in front of him. "*No*," she screamed. "Don't leave me alone again, say something to me, anything!"

Billy grasped her shoulders and easily lifted her aside. "Goodnight, Mary."

Mary felt herself crumble, her last resistance to Billy's indifference having exhausted itself.

She fell onto the floor, sobbing with such sadness that she felt her very heart would break.

Billy stepped over her prone body and went to bed, closing the door quietly behind him.

Finally, the sobbing stopped and Mary hauled herself onto her bed. She wasn't without sin, but she didn't deserve to be punished like this. "God help me," she pleaded. "Please, God, help me."

The following day, Billy left for work as usual, making no reference to the night before. He kissed Nancy goodbye. "Daddy'll be home tonight," he told her. "And I'll read you one of your stories."

Mary sat like stone, watching the display of affection. "Is there no story for me then?" she asked. "No kiss goodbye?"

The door of the kitchen closed in silence.

She nearly didn't hear the soft knock at the door at midday and almost like a puppet she turned the handle and opened it.

John Anderson stood before her.

"Mary?" he asked his voice full of concern. "What's happened to you?"

Mary felt as though she was seeing John Anderson through a long tunnel. "John," she whispered in disbelief. "Is that you?"

John Anderson stepped towards her and wrapped his arms around her, holding her close to him.

"Where have you been Mary?" he whispered his voice trembling with relief. "I've been going out of my mind wondering if you were alright."

Mary held on to him, hearing only his voice and allowing it to seep into her soul.

"He forbade me," she told him haltingly. "He wants to punish me for…"

John Anderson held her tighter. "Punish you for what, Mary? What does he think you've done?"

Mary's empty eyes gazed at him. "I killed his child."

John Anderson slowly released her.

"Nancy?" he asked, his voice hoarse with disbelief.

Mary shook her head. "No, not Nancy," she whispered. "His unborn child," she told him, beyond caring.

John led her to a chair and sat her down. "You're not making sense, Mary. Tell me from the beginning."

In a monotone voice, Mary slowly told John everything, of the night Billy took her against her will, of the fear she felt of him, of her terror in finding she was pregnant with his child and her decision to end the pregnancy. John listened with patience and concern.

"Why didn't you let me know?" he asked her.

Mary's eyes levelled with his. "And what could you have done, John? Taken me away from all this?"

John grasped both her hands in his. "Yes," he answered simply.

Mary felt a small flame of hope ignite in her heart. She looked at him in disbelief.

"And Isabella?" she asked. "What about Isabella?"

John Anderson bowed his head. "I'm not proud of myself, Mary, but these last few months have shown me that living a lie isn't the answer. I've prayed to God to show me a way and I've tried to forget you. Isabella's a good woman, Mary, but I don't love her. I love you."

Mary felt all her limbs tremble. "Oh! John!" she exclaimed, tears spilling from her eyes. "Then don't leave me here with Billy… please."

John soothed her fears. "It's alright," he whispered. "I won't leave you again, but I have to make arrangements for us to be together. Wait a little longer for me my dearest and remember I love you with all my heart."

For a long time after he left, Mary held on to his words. "He'll be back," she told herself. "He loves me." She picked up Nancy and hugged her soft body, swaying from side to side as she did so.

The stirring of her child brought her back to reality. Billy would never let her take Nancy from him, never. She held the child tightly to her as new fears replaced the old.

She would speak to Annie. She'd know what to do. Mary gathered up Nancy and ran down the stair with her to the end of the close, to await Annie's return from the mill.

Annie spied her figure pacing up and down on the pavement as she turned into the lane. Instinctively, Annie knew something was wrong.

"What is it, Mary?" she asked, hurrying towards her. "Is it Billy?"

"No Annie," she told her, trying to keep the agitation out of her voice. "It's not Billy. I've had a visitor."

Annie's eyes levelled with her sister's. "Who?" she asked quietly.

Mary's eyes flickered skywards unable to hold Annie's gaze. "John Anderson."

Annie hurried her and Nancy along the close to her door. "And what did John Anderson have to say?" she asked, turning the key in the lock and letting the three of them inside.

Mary placed Nancy on the floor, where she immediately began to toddle about inspecting everything moveable.

"He's asked me to go away with him," she said, trying to keep control of her fears.

Annie stopped what she was doing. "You refused, of course?" It was part question, part statement.

Mary's chin began to quiver. "Oh, Annie, please don't tell me to stay with Billy. You don't know what he's like. He never speaks to me, Annie, never sleeps with me… Oh! Annie, please, please don't tell me to stay." Mary crumpled into a small heap of misery and, once again, Annie responded to her sister's despair.

"Mary, Mary," she coaxed. "Come on, there's no need for all this. Billy's your husband, you've a lovely daughter and there's no reason to go."

Mary's emotions spilled over. "I *hate* him, Annie, I *hate* him. John's going to come back for me and we're going away together. Don't ask me to stay…" Mary dissolved into a fresh flood of tears.

Fear gripped Annie's heart. Billy was a proud man. He wouldn't take kindly to another man replacing him in the affections of his wife and especially not of his child. Annie's thoughts froze.

"What's going to happen to Nancy?" she asked Mary, concern mounting for her sister and her child. "Billy loves his daughter, anyone can see that. Mary, it'll break his heart if he loses Nancy."

Mary stared at the gas lamp as it hissed and glowed. "I can't bear any more Annie," she announced in a small voice. "If I can't be with John… I'll kill myself."

Annie knew she meant it.

A week later, Annie was wakened by a loud banging at her door.

She leapt from her bed and ran to the window. Billy's figure was leaning heavily against the lintel as his hand pounded incessantly.

"Where is she?" he demanded in a loud voice. "I know she's in there, Annie Pepper. Send her out."

Annie tried to calm him. "Billy, she's not here, I swear," she told him, her mind trying to assimilate what had happened. "Come in and look for yourself."

A few neighbours stuck their heads out of their windows or leant over the railings of the walkways.

"What's all the racket, then?" asked one. "Anybody would think it was Hogmanay."

Annie tried to usher Billy inside. "I'm sorry," called Annie in return. "Just a misunderstanding."

She got Billy inside and sat him down beside the fire. "Please calm down Billy," she asked plaintively. "You can see Mary's not here."

Billy looked as though he were carved from granite. "Where is she Annie?" he asked. "I know she'd tell you. Now, you tell *me*."

Annie tried to gain some time to gather her thoughts. "Tell me what's happened Billy and I'll do everything I can to help."

Billy 's eyes narrowed. "She's left me and Nancy."

Annie felt her blood run cold. "She's left Nancy?" she asked incredulously. "No Billy, not that."

Billy remained motionless. "What's his name, Annie?"

Annie felt her whole body strain with the duplicity of it all. "John Anderson," she replied anxiously. "She says you don't love her any more Billy and that she can't live the lie any longer."

"She's my *wife*," exploded Billy. "Doesn't that mean anything anymore?"

Annie reached out for his hand but he drew it away from her.

"I sacrificed everything for her," he whispered hoarsely. "And what do I get in return?"

Annie sat motionless.

"*Nothing*," he shouted, towering over her, his eyes blazing with disillusionment and hurt. Billy slumped back into the chair. "Nothing," he repeated, tears beginning to trickle down his face.

Annie felt her heart reach out for him.

"You still have Nancy," she reminded him. "You still have your beautiful daughter."

Billy's eyes blazed. "All I ever wanted was you."

Annie's emotions were in turmoil. "Well, that's as maybe," she whispered. "Some things just aren't meant to be." Billy hung his head, its weight carrying his shoulders with it.

"Help me Annie," he asked. "I don't care about Mary, but Nancy, what's to become of her?"

Annie knew immediately what he was thinking. "I can't replace Mary as Nancy's mother, Billy," she said quietly, turning away from him. "Don't ask me to do that."

Billy, suddenly realising he had a chance to trap Annie in his world, stood up and turned her to face him. "I'll pay you Annie," he begged. "You know I will."

Annie felt herself weaken. "But what about my job?" she responded shakily, searching for a reason to refuse, but knowing she couldn't turn her back on Mary's child.

Billy placed his hands on her shoulders suddenly seeing the silver lining in his cloud of despair. "You can work part-time, if you like," he told her. "I'll clear it with Campbell. Mrs Ogilvie can mind Nancy in the mornings and you can take over at dinnertime." His fingers gripped her shoulders tighter. "Say yes, Annie," he implored. "Please, say *yes*."

Annie felt her resolve disappear. "As long as I can live in my home and only look after Nancy in the afternoons, then… I'll do it."

Billys eyes suddenly caught light. "Annie, oh! Annie, you won't regret it, I promise you." He resisted the urge to throw his arms around her and instead, stepped back from her and clenched his hands behind his back. "I'll see Mrs Ogilvie tomorrow," he told her, Mary already seemingly forgotten. "She's a good woman and she'll take care of Nancy till you come home."

Annie nodded. "I'll collect her from Mrs Ogilvie at one o'clock then," she told Billy.

Billy nodded. "One o'clock," he repeated. "And I'll see you at seven."

Annie returned to her bed, her mind in turmoil. 'What happened to Mary?' she wondered. 'Has she really gone off with John Anderson and left Billy and Nancy? And why have I agreed to step into her shoes?' She hoped that the morning would bring some sense into her world, as sleep eluded her that night.

The following day, she reported for duty at the mill. Billy immediately came over to her looms.

"It's all arranged," he told her. "Mrs Ogilvie's looking after Nancy till you collect her and Mr Campbell's agreed to your working part-time for a while, due to the circumstances."

Annie felt as if she'd been steamrollered into her new lifestyle, but it also seemed the natural thing to do, looking after her sister's child. 'But where *is* Mary?' she wondered. and how long would it be before guilt made her return for Nancy?

Annie duly arrived to pick up her niece at the appointed hour.

Mrs Ogilvie opened the door. "I've come for Nancy," she said. "Is she alright?"

The minder signalled Annie to follow her into the house.

"She's done nothing but girn for her mum," announced Grannie Ogilvie. "She's missin' her something terrible."

Nancy's eyes lit up on seeing Annie. "Nannie," she squealed. "Mummy, mummy?"

Annie picked her up. "Nannie's going to look after you for a while, Nancy, till mummy comes back."

Nancy's face fell. "Da da?" she called. "Da da?"

Annie hugged her closely. "Thanks Mrs Ogilvie," she said. "I'll take care of her now."

"We'll see you tomorrow then?" she queried. Annie nodded and hurried Nancy from the house.

"How could Mary desert her daughter?" she asked herself. "And such a beautiful child as Nancy."

Once home, Nancy seemed to settle and Annie busied herself about the kitchen, preparing an evening meal for Billy and chatting to her niece.

"Daddy'll be home soon," she told her, as she sat on Annie's lap ready for bed.

"Me 'tory?" she asked Annie.

"Yes child," replied Annie. "Daddy'll tell you a nice story when he comes home."

Her thoughts turned to her own child, somewhere in Ireland, growing up without her.

Billy's child too and a son. Annie fought back the tears.

"It wasn't meant to be like this," She thought aloud. "Where did it all go wrong?"

Billy arrived home on the dot at seven.

It was a long time since he'd wanted to come home, never mind relish the prospect.

Annie was sitting with Nancy as he entered the kitchen.

He could feel his throat tighten with desire for her. "Are you alright?" he asked.

Annie rose and held Nancy out to him. "She's grieving, Billy," she said solemnly. "She wants her mother."

Billy held Nancy aloft. "Where's daddy's girl then?" he smiled. Nancy gurgled with pleasure.

"There," he said. "She's fine Annie, just fine."

"She wants her mother," Annie repeated. "She wants Mary."

Billy clenched his jaw and set Nancy down on the floor.

"Well, she can't have her, can she?" His eyes were bleak with confusion. "It wasn't me who left," he stated. "It was her."

Annie nodded. "I know, Billy," she agreed. "But she must have been desperately unhappy to have left Nancy."

Billy sniffed the air. "Something smells good," he said. "Is that for me?"

Annie sighed. "Yes, Billy, it's for you. A man can't work all day and come home to nothing," she replied. "And anyway, Nancy needs to be fed as much as you."

"Will you stay?" he asked meekly. "And eat with us?"

Annie hesitated. "No thanks, Billy," she said. "I've my own tea to see to at home."

Unwilling to pursue his cause too soon, Billy stepped back and indicated the door. "Well," he said. "thanks for everything, Annie, and I'll see you tomorrow."

Annie walked quickly past him. "Tomorrow," she replied. "Goodnight Nancy."

Nancy squealed "Nannie!"

Back in her own room, Annie had time to think.

She could see the future as plain as she could see the black kettle on the range.

With Mary gone, Billy would pursue her more and more and with Nancy as the link; she felt herself being pulled inexorably by an ever-tightening chain which ultimately would lead to Billy.

"Where *is* Mary," she called angrily into the silence. "She's no right to do this to me. Wasn't it enough that she took Billy from me in the first place without leaving me to pick up the pieces of her broken marriage?" Annie poked the fire till the sparks flew up the chimney and the face of Joe Cassiday shimmered in the flames. "Where are you Joe?" she wept. "Didn't you love me truly?"

Joe's form blurred into fire again as Annie swung the kettle over the heat and made herself some tea. She cut two thick slices of bread and held them on the toasting fork to brown at the flames and wondered how long it would be before the whole neighbourhood knew about her sister an John Anderson.

Jessie met her at the mill gate the following morning.

"Annie," she called. "Where did you go yesterday?"

Annie joined her on the walk to the weaving flat. "Mary's left Billy," she announced. "And I'm minding Nancy."

Jessie stopped dead in her tracks. "*Left her bairn*?" she repeated. "What kind of a woman is your sister, Annie?"

Annie inhaled deeply. "Don't condemn her Jessie, please," she asked. "I don't know what drove her to it, but it must have been unbearable, for her to go."

Jessie sighed and nodded sagely. "I've known misery, Annie and I've known hunger, but never, never, would I leave the bairns."

"I know," agreed Annie, wanting the conversation to end. "I know. But she's gone, Jessie, whether we like it or not, and I can't turn my back on her child."

"You're a brave lassie, Annie Pepper," Jessie told her. "I just hope that sister of yours comes to her senses soon."

Annie's shoulders drooped in despair. "Pray for us Jessie," she asked. "When next you're at the Salvation Army meeting."

Jessie pulled her shoulders back and straightened her head. "I'll do that, Annie lass, don't you worry. I'm going the night."

Annie knew that Jessie would hear about John Anderson's disappearance that night. News like that always travelled fastest and it was only a matter of time before she'd have to tell Jessie the truth. Annie was waiting for her the next day and Jessie lost no time in recounting the Captain's mysterious disappearance.

"Everybody's saying he's run off with another woman," she whispered, relishing the scandal. "But nobody knows who!"

"I know," Annie told Jessie, her voice heavy with resignation. "The woman he's ran off with is my sister… Mary."

Jessie stood motionless for several seconds trying to take in Annie's words. "Mary!" she echoed, the sparkle going out of her voice. Annie nodded.

"So that's how you're having to mind her bairn?"

"Yes Jessie," Annie replied. "Grannie Ogilvie minds her in the morning and I take over for the rest of the day. Billy's arranged part-time work for me with Mr Campbell, till things get sorted out."

Jessie shook her head sadly. "Of course." She nodded. "It's all you can do. Oh, Annie, how could she?" Annie hung her head, feeling her sister's shame for her.

"And Isabella Anderson's such a fine woman as well," Jessie added. "God, Annie, what's wrong with that sister of yours then?" she asked, more to herself than Annie. "She leaves her wee lassie and breaks up two marriages!" Jessie's voice was rising with incredulity.

Annie stifled a sob which threatened to push its way out. "I know, I know," she whispered. "I'm not proud of what she's done, Jessie, but she's still my sister and Nancy's still my niece."

Annie pulled herself up to her full height. "And before anyone asks," she added. "I'm not living at her house with her husband - I'm there to look after Nancy and nothing else."

Jessie knew not to pursue the conversation further. "Oh, Annie, I never thought for a minute…"

"I don't mean you Jessie, I mean all the rest who'll be quick to blacken my name."

The two women walked in silence into the weaving flat. Every eye in the place watched Annie as she began work and many knowing nods and looks were passed behind her back.

Time weighed heavily till the one o'clock hooter sounded signalling dinnertime and Annie was able to escape the atmosphere which had developed around her.

She ran quickly to Mrs Ogilvie's to collect Nancy. "C'mon little one," she called softly. "Nannie's here." Mrs Ogilvie emerged from her kitchen. "There's somebody wants to see you," she announced, stepping aside to reveal the figure of Isabella Anderson.

Annie felt sick with apprehension. "Isabella!" It was obvious from her eyes that she'd been crying and Annie knew exactly how she felt.

"I live at the far end of the close," Annie murmured. "I'll make us some tea, if you'd like." Isabella's chin began to tremble and she was unable to speak, but she stood up and followed Annie to her door in silence.

Annie sat Nancy down to play with her peg doll. "The tea will only be a minute," she said quietly. Annie could feel Isabella's distress come at her in waves.

The sound of the liquid hitting the cups emphasised the silence. She passed her a cup of tea which was taken with trembling hands.

"Where are they?" she asked Annie in a tiny, broken voice. "Please tell me."

"I don't know Isabella," she replied. "If I did, believe me, I'd tell you." Isabella's shoulders heaved in a new wave of tears. Annie knelt by her. "I'm so sorry, Isabella," she whispered. "So very sorry."

"I thought we had the happiest of marriages," she managed to say between sobs. "I never imagined… this." Her eyes, red-rimmed and clouded, suddenly levelled with Annie's. "You *must* have known what was happening," Isabella quivered. "You're her *sister*!"

Annie flinched. "I know Billy and her weren't getting on," she told Isabella. "But I never thought she'd leave him, nor her little girl. As far as I know, she hadn't been out of the house for weeks, except to buy the messages, so whatever happened, Isabella, it must have happened a while ago, but I know no more than that."

Just as a fresh wave of tears threatened to engulf Isabella again, there was a knock at the door. Annie answered it quickly, frightened it might be Billy.

The tall figure of a man stood before her. He bent slightly to speak to her, his voice low but clear. "Mrs Ogilvie says my sister's here." Annie nodded and stepped back to allow him to enter.

As soon as Isabella saw him, the flood of tears began. "Alex, Alex," she wept. "Help me."

"Hush now, Isabella, I'm here now, it's alright." He held her gently till the sobbing eased.

"I'll take her home now," he said to Annie. "But I'd like to speak to your brother-in-law sometime soon. Perhaps you could tell him that Alexander Melville will be calling later this evening.

Annie nodded. "He lives on the top landing," she told him and he'll be home about seven. I'll tell him to expect you." Alexander Melville thanked her and guided his sister out of Annie's kitchen. "I believe you're the sister. Annie is it?" he asked.

"Yes," Annie nodded wearily. "I'm the sister, Annie."

On Billy's return, Annie explained about his impending visitor. "I don't exactly know what he wants," she told Billy. "But he's Isabella Anderson's brother, I think you must see him."

Billy was reluctant to speak to anyone about his wife's shame and wasn't looking forward to meeting Alexander Melville at all.

At the appointed hour, the visitor arrived and Annie made to leave. "Please." He held up his hand. "There's no need to leave, in fact, it may help if you stay."

Annie looked at Billy, who nodded and she sat down on the spindle chair beside the kitchen table.

"Perhaps I should introduce myself fully," he began. "I'm Alexander Melville, Isabella's brother and I'm a policeman with the Dundee Constabulary. Right at this moment, there are people out searching for them, Mr Dawson," he said to Billy. "Obviously that's unofficial, but it would make it easier if you could give me an indication of where you think they might be."

Billy folded his arms. "If I knew where the pair of them were, do you really think I'd be sitting here?"

Alexander nodded. "I suppose not," he said. "But I had to ask."

"Is Isabella feeling any better?" Annie enquired. Two clear blue eyes looked at her, full of concern and worry. He shook his head. "I don't know if she'll ever get over this."

Billy grunted.

"If we find them," asked Alexander. "Do you want your wife back?"

"*No*," Billy almost shouted. "I want nothing more to do with that whore."

Annie drew back at the insult to her sister and anger flared inside her. "She's no *whore*, Billy Dawson. She may not be perfect, but she's not that." Annie's eyes blurred with tears.

"Please Mr Dawson," interjected Alex Melville. "It's an upsetting time for all of us, but language like that isn't going to help."

"I'm sorry, Annie," Billy muttered. "You've been an angel through all this and I don't want you upset as well."

"I'd best be going," she told him stoutly. "And don't paint everyone with the same black brush, Billy, not unless you're going to include yourself in the picture."

Alex stood back and let her pass. "I'll be going as well, Mr Dawson," he added, turning up the collar of his coat. "Thanks for seeing me." He followed Annie out onto the landing and down the stairwell to her house.

"It's a bad business," he commented. "If I hear anything, I'll let you know.

Annie smiled weakly. "It would have been better if it had never happened."

"Will you be alright?" Alex asked. "It seems to me you've been handed a heavy burden."

Annie raised her eyes to the heavens and blinked at the moon. "Do you ever wish you could go for a walk and just keep walking?" she asked him. "Till you've left all your burdens behind."

Alex smiled. "Aye, Annie, I know what you mean. My own wife died last year of the fever and I wanted to walk away then." His eyes clouded with the memory. "Isabella got me though that time, Annie, and that's why I'm here for her now."

Annie reached out and touched his arm. "I'm sorry," she said gently. "I didn't know."

Alex patted her hand. "We're two orphans of the storm, Annie, me and you. But we're made of stern stuff, we Irish."

Annie's eyes opened in amazement. "But you don't sound Irish."

Alex laughed. "On the mammy's side," he told her, feigning an Irish voice. "But the rest of me is as Scottish as it gets."

For a moment, in the moonlight, a little laughter entered their lives. Alex bowed his head slightly and said goodnight. "I'll speak to you again, Annie," he told her. "And let's hope this sorry business is sorted soon."

Annie closed the door and slumped onto her bed. She was too tired to eat and fell asleep even without changing into her night things.

CHAPTER 14

It was two weeks later when the letter arrived, written in Mary's childlike hand. Annie hurriedly opened it.

'Dear Annie' it began, 'John and me are in Edinburgh. I'm sorry about everything, Annie, look after Nancy for me. Please don't tell Billy. Love, Mary.'

Annie clasped the letter to her breast. "Edinburgh," she gasped. She scanned the words again for any clues of where in Edinburgh, Mary might be, but there was none. At least she was safe.

Annie paced up and down the floor trying to decide what to do for the best. It would be foolish to tell Billy and she didn't want to cause Isabella any more distress. She would tell Alex Melville, she decided, wrapping her shawl around her shoulders and pulling on her work boots. Once he knew Mary and John were in Edinburgh, maybe he would be able to find them. As soon as her shift was over at the mill she would pick up Nancy and find the policeman.

With her niece toddling beside her she made her way to the Police Station at the end of Bell Street where it joined the road to the small settlement called Lochee.

She could hear voices behind a door with a frosted glass window and knocked on the pane. There was a shuffling of paper and feet before the door was opened by a uniformed policeman.

He looked at Annie and then Nancy. "And what can we do for you, young lady?" he smiled, bending down to pick up Nancy.

"What a bonny bairn," he indicated to Annie. "Is she yours?"

"She's my sister's child," Annie told him. "I'm looking after her for a while."

The policeman nodded and, placing Nancy back on her feet, turned his attention back to Annie.

"I'm wanting to speak to Mr Melville," she said. "I'm not sure if it's here I'll find him, but I don't know where he lives and he said he was a policeman and…" The constable held up his hand to stop her babble.

"Slow down," he said. "Slow down. Now, Sergeant Melville is on duty at this station," he told Annie. "But he's not due to start till three o'clock."

"What time is it now?"

The policemen looked back through the door to a large clock on the wall. "It's only just past two o'clock."

"Can I wait?" asked Annie.

The policemen looked at Nancy and ruffled the curls on her head. "Only if she's a good girl," he told Annie.

Annie pulled Nancy close to her knee. "She'll be no bother, sir," she said. "No bother at all."

The policeman nodded. "You can wait here then."

The frosted glass door closed, once more confining the activity behind it only to those within.

At five minutes past three, Alex Melville, in his Sergeant's uniform, emerged through the door. He always impressed everyone who saw him and Annie was no exception. Three stripes flashed on the arm of his tunic and the buttons shone. If anything, he was even taller than Annie remembered and his moustached face was topped with brown wavy hair which, despite obvious attempts to tame it, continued to form curls along the hairline of his brow.

He immediately came towards her, his face etched with concern. "Annie. What brings you here? Is there news?"

Annie pulled the letter from her skirt pocket. "This came today."

Alex read it carefully. "Edinburgh!" he muttered. "Now that makes sense."

Annie looked perplexed. "Why?" she asked.

"John's from Edinburgh," he told her. "Looks like he's gone back to the place he knows best."

"Then, you know where he'll be?"

"Possibly, Annie," Alex replied. "Can I keep this just now?" He held up the letter.

Annie nodded. "If you think it'll do any good."

"I'm sorry you've been kept waiting so long," Alex added. "Has anyone given you a cup of tea?" Annie shook her head. "Then come with me."

Annie and Nancy followed him through the frosted glass door and into a large room.

The policeman who had first spoken to her was seated behind a desk, writing and behind him hung rows of iron keys on a wooden board. Alex noticed her looking at them.

"They're cell keys," he told her in reply to her unasked question. "Constable McPherson here's responsible for making sure everyone's locked up safely." He nodded towards a solid oak door with a tiny iron grill set into it.

Alex handed her a mug of tea and Nancy a cup of milk. "Don't look so worried, Annie." He smiled. "We only lock people up who deserve it."

Annie sipped the hot tea. She'd never been in a jail before was glad there was a stout door between her and its inmates.

"Do you really think you'll find them?" she asked, handing back the empty mug.

"Question is, Annie," he replied. "What happens when we *do* find them?"

"Billy won't have Mary back," Annie said. "That's for certain, and I don't know what he'd do if he came face to face with John Anderson."

"Isabella would have John back in a minute," he continued. "As far as she's concerned, he's her husband till death do them part."

Annie sighed. "Will you tell her he's in Edinburgh?"

"Not yet, I don't think, not till I know exactly where they are and I've spoken to them both."

Annie looked at the clock. "Is that the time?" she asked anxiously. Alex nodded.

"Billy will be home before I've had the chance to get his tea ready," she exclaimed. "And he'll want to know where I've been…" She began to pull the bemused Nancy towards the door.

"Calm down, Annie," Alex told her. "Everything'll be alright."

Annie caught her breath. "Everything'll be alright," she repeated nodding and, somehow, he made it sound as though it would.

He placed his hands on her shoulders. "You've been a tower of strength, Annie," he told her softly. "You're not going to break now."

Annie could feel the warmth of his hands through the fabric of her blouse and, for a moment, felt utterly safe, a feeling she hadn't experienced since the death of her father.

"I'll let you know where they are, as soon as I know," Alex said. "But if there's anything else happens to worry you, you know where I am."

"Thanks," she replied simply, bending down and sweeping Nancy into her arms. "And thanks for the tea."

Alex gave her a mock salute. "All part of the service, madam."

For the second time since they met, laughter again entered their lives.

Billy was becoming increasingly morose at Annie's lack of response to his advances. He had hoped that, with Mary gone, it would have been an easy matter for him to convince Annie that they should rekindle their love for one another, but things weren't working out as he had expected.

For a start, Annie had stuck to the times she looked after Nancy and as soon as Billy returned from work, she would go. She had refused to eat with him and rebuffed any attempts by him to get closer to her.

"Mrs Ogilvie," Billy asked politely one Friday morning as he dropped off Nancy. "I hope it's not out of order to ask this, but would it be possible for you to look after Nancy this Saturday for me? I've several things I need to attend to and…"

"Say no more, Mr Dawson," she interrupted. "Just let me know what time you'll be wanting to come back for her. But, you realise it'll be more expensive for Saturdays."

Billy nodded in agreement. "Naturally, Mrs Ogilvie, just name your price."

"Two shillings for all day and half a crown if it goes past six o'clock."

"A very fair price," said Billy, handing Mrs Ogilvie a two shilling piece and a sixpence.

She sniffed as she pocketed the coins. "It'll be a long day then?" she queried.

"Just in case," added Billy. "Sometimes things take longer than you first expect."

Mrs Ogilvie closed the door and through the netting of her kitchen curtains, she watched Blly go.

"And what's your daddy up to then?" she asked Nancy, removing the child's coat.

"Da da?" repeated the child. "Da da?"

Billy had decided that today was the day he was going to finally convince Annie of his sincerity. As the Saturday dawned, however, Nancy was fretting and no matter what Billy did, she continued to whimper.

"C'mon Nancy, there's a good girl," he pleaded. "Mrs Ogilvie's got a gingerbread man for you."

Nancy burst into tears. "No," she cried. "No go."

Billy snatched her up into his arms in desperation. "Oh, yes you are, young lady," he told his daughter. "That's if you want Auntie Annie to come and stay with us."

At the mention of Annie's name, Nancy brightened.

"There, you see," Billy scolded her. "There's nothing wrong with you at all."

He deposited the protesting Nancy with Mrs Ogilvie and breathed a sigh of relief as he made his way to Annie's door.

"Can I come in?" he asked, as the door was opened to him.

Annie sensed a difference in him. An excitement even. "Is everything alright?" she asked cautiously.

"Never better," Billy replied. "Can I come in?"

Annie stood aside and allowed him to pass.

"Well?" she asked apprehensively.

"Why Annie, don't look so worried. I've just come to take you out."

Annie frowned. "Take me out where?" she asked suspiciously.

"Anywhere!" Billy replied. "I just want to show my appreciation for all you've done for Nancy since Mary's been gone and…" his show of lightness began to falter. "Please, Annie, come out with me?"

Annie saw the tension in his stance and the glint of anxiety in his eyes.

"I don't think so, Billy," she replied, turning away from him. "I've a lot to do today," she added, trying to think of a way of getting him to leave.

Billy caught her arm and swung her round to face him. "Don't turn away from me, Annie," he ordered her, his features hardening and sweat forming on his upper lip. "I only want to please you."

Annie's felt her legs begin to tremble as she faced him. "If you want to please me," she whispered, "Then you'll go."

Billy pulled her towards him. "You wouldn't be saying that if I were Joe Cassiday, now would you?"

Annie began to struggle to free herself but Billy's grip tightened.

"*Get out,*" she screamed. "And stay away from me."

Her whole body was shaking now as the remembered fear of their last encounter gripped her.

Billy suddenly released her. "You've got it wrong, Annie," he whispered hoarsely. "I only want to show you how much I still love you."

Annie's heart was pounding. "Don't talk like that Billy," she begged. "Just *go*, please."

For what seemed like an eternity, Billy stared at her. "Alright Annie," he finally conceded. "I'll go. But I don't give up that easily. I'll be back for you and I'll keep coming back for you till you're mine."

There was no mistaking the obsession in his voice and for a long time after he'd gone, Annie felt unable to move, staring at the fire till the flames turned to a glow. Eventually, she swung the kettle over the heat and made some tea, sipping it slowly to calm herself.

"Please God, send Mary back," she murmured to herself. It was the only way she could see that would free her from Billy.

Stung by Annie's rejection, Billy headed for the only place he knew where he'd not be rejected. The Thrums Bar. The Landlord welcomed him with a smile.

"Well, well, Mr Dawson, we haven't seen you round here for a while. What can I get you?"

Billy leaned against the mahogany bar and pointed to a beer barrel. "Beer," he ordered. "And a whisky."

The barman glanced at the Landlord, who nodded.

"Everything alright?" he asked mildly.

Billy clenched his jaw. "No," he replied, downing the whisky and gulping a mouthful of the beer. "But it soon will be."

Billy nodded imperceptibly to the barman. "Same again."

It took a long time before the alcohol finally dulled Billy's mind.

The Landlord had been watching him carefully. He'd seen Billy drunk before, but not like this. There was a stillness about him which unnerved him. He indicated to the barman to stop serving him.

"Time to go home, Billy," the landlord told him amiably, as he tried to order another whisky.

Billy's eyes were like black coals glittering in the lights of the bar, as two barmen took him by the elbow to lead him to the door.

"Get your hands *off* me," he spat, his words seeming to come from the depth of his soul.

"Now, Mr Dawson," said the Landlord. "We only want to make sure you get home alright."

"*Home*?" shouted Billy. "What's *that*?"

The barmen tightened their grip on his arms as the landlord looked to one of his regulars. "Fetch the bobbies," he ordered. "He's not going to go quietly."

Jimmy Burns nodded his head and scuttled out the door.

"Sent for the *police*, have you," Billy bawled. "Well they'll not take *me*, not Billy Dawson."

Glasses went crashing to the floor as Billy struggled to free himself. One of the barmen fell backwards sending bottles and pints spilling in all directions and customers scurried for the exit.

Billy could hear the police whistles getting louder and struggled even more.

"*You bastards!*" he roared. "ANNIE!"

Two burly policemen caught him as he fell forward. "Now then sir," said one. "Just come quietly with us and we'll make sure you get a good night's sleep."

Billy gazed up at them through blurred vision. "Annie," he whispered hoarsely. "Tell Annie."

Alex Melville was on duty when Billy was brought in.

"Drunk and Disorderly, Sergeant," announced the Constable. "Thrums Bar in King Street."

"Lock him up then," Alex instructed Constable McPherson. "We'll see what he has to say for himself in the morning."

"I'll just get his details first, Sergeant."

"No need," Alex replied. "I know who he is."

Constable McPherson shrugged his shoulders. "Right, Sergeant," he nodded. "Anything you say."

Alex Melville looked at the clock. "Ewan," he called down the passageway leading to the cells. Constable McPherson's head popped round the side of a cell door.

"Yes, Sergeant?"

"Look after the shop for a while," he asked. "There's something I've got to do."

The constable nodded. "Right you are."

Alex donned his overcoat and turned up the collar, bracing himself against the north wind that signalled the onset of winter. He hurried along Bell Street and up Victoria Road to the top of William Lane. He could see a light burning in Annie's window from the top of the steps and covered them two at a time.

Knocking on her door he softly called her name. "Annie, it's me, Alex Melville."

Annie opened the door and he could see the whiteness of her face.

"Thank God," she whispered. "I thought you were Billy come back."

"Come back?" he asked gently. "Can I come in?"

Annie nodded. "He was here earlier… he wanted me to…" The memory of Billy agitated her emotions and she began to tremble again.

Alex put her arm around her and led her to a chair. "There, there, sit here."

Annie's throat tightened with tears preventing her from speaking.

Alex Melville, his hand stroking her shoulders, hushed her like a child till the shaking stopped.

"He won't stop bothering me…" she mumbled. "He just won't stop."

Alex knelt down beside her. "He's in jail, Annie."

Annie gasped. "*Jail?*"

Alex nodded. "He was arrested tonight. Drunk and disorderly."

Annie leapt from the chair. "*Nancy,*" she exclaimed, "*Where's Nancy?*" She raced out of the door and up the stairs to her sister's house. "*Nancy,*" she called. "NANCY." But the door was locked and there was no sign of life.

Mrs Ogilvie's door opened. "What's all the shouting about?" she demanded. "There's bairns trying to sleep in here."

Annie ran towards her. "Mrs Ogilvie, is Nancy with you?"

The old woman nodded. "Aye, Master Dawson left her with me the day. Said he'd be back for her later. But I didn't expect it would be as late as this."

Annie breathed a sigh of relief. "Is she alright with you for the night Mrs Ogilvie?"

"I suppose so," she sniffed. "But it'll cost another shilling."

"Thanks Mrs Ogilvie," Annie replied. "I'll make sure you're paid."

Alex Melville was waiting at the foot of the stairs. "She's with Mrs Ogilvie?" he queried.

"Yes," replied Annie. "I'll get her tomorrow."

"Could you use some good news, Annie?"

Annie looked at him.

"I've found John and Mary, and I've spoken to them."

Annie could hardly believe her ears. She pulled him back to her room. "Tell me, quickly, how's Mary? When is she coming back? Is she well?"

"One question at a time, *please?*" Alex smiled.

Annie felt herself relax. "I'm sorry," she said. "It's just that Mary coming back would solve so much."

"I thought Billy didn't want her back?" he asked.

"No, he doesn't, but Nancy does. She's missing her something dreadful."

"Mary's missing Nancy too," Alex responded. "It's a bit of a mess, isn't it?"

Annie bit her lip. "Is she happy?"

Alex shrugged. "How can she be?" he said. "Not knowing how her daughter is."

"And John, how's he?"

"No one in the Army will speak to him," he said bluntly. "They've paid a terrible price for their love, Annie."

"What's to be done, Alex?"

"I'm taking Isabella through to Edinburgh tomorrow. I think you and Nancy should come too."

"To Edinburgh," Annie echoed.

"It might make the difference," he said.

"What about Billy?"

"It'll be Monday before he's released and we'll be back by then."

Annie nodded in agreement.

"Isabella and me will meet you at the East Station at nine o'clock. And don't worry about the fare," he added. "I'll pay it."

"Alright, Alex, I'll see you tomorrow."

"And don't worry," said Alex. "Everything'll be alright."

Annie suddenly felt safe again, only this time, the feeling was stronger.

CHAPTER 15

The train puffed across the Tay Bridge and wound its way through the Fife countryside into mid-Lothian. Isabella Anderson seemed calm and almost detached as she gazed out of the window at the passing landscape.

"Thank you for allowing me to come," Annie said. Isabella turned to face her. "I've no quarrel with you Annie," she responded, tonelessly. "Nor with Mary, really, I just want my husband back."

She turned again to the window and her thoughts and they all fell into silence till the train pulled into Waverley Station.

Edinburgh thronged with people. Annie gazed at the castle from Princess Street, as she and Nancy followed Alex and Isabella through the crowds. Flags seemed to be everywhere, billowing in the stiff Easterly wind and mixing with the noise of horses' hooves and street traders voices.

"Where are we going?" Annie called to Alex's back.

"Leith," came back the answer.

"Leith," Annie repeated to herself, hoping it would conjure up an image of Mary's new life, but nothing came. They left Princes Street behind as the road to Leith Docks dipped downhill before them. Nancy was tired after the long train journey and began dragging her feet.

"C'mon Nancy," beckoned Annie, opening her arms. "Auntie Annie'll carry you for a bit."

But the strong hand of Alex Melville held her back. "Here," he said gently. "Let me." He swept Nancy up onto his shoulders. "There," he laughed. "She'll see the whole of Edinburgh from up there." Nancy clutched his hair with her hands and gurgled with glee.

Annie fell in step with Isabella as Alex strode out. "Are you alright, Isabella?" she asked.

Isabella drew a deep breath. "I just want him back, Annie," she said simply. "God knows my love for him and..."her voice began to falter. "And I just want him back."

The narrow wooden stair to the attic flat where Mary and John Anderson had taken lodgings, creaked under the weight of Alex Melville. He turned and looked back at Annie. "Alright?" he asked. Annie nodded. He knocked loudly on the door at the top.

It opened and John Anderson, his face gaunt and his lanky frame even thinner, stood before them.

"Come in, Alex," he murmured. "We've been expecting you back."

Alex entered, followed by Annie carrying Nancy, then Isabella.

On seeing her daughter, Mary let out a whoop of delight and ran towards her. "*Nancy*, where's my little girl?" She hugged the child to her and reached out her hand to Annie. "Thank you, Annie, for looking after her."

Annie stood back to allow Isabella Anderson into the room. The blood seemed to drain from John Anderson's face at the sight of her.

"Isabella!" he whispered. Isabella's eyes clouded with tears as she looked around the attic room.

"Is this what you've come to?" she asked him quietly. John wiped a sudden tear from his eye.

Alex moved between him and Isabella. "I think Isabella's got something she wants to say to you... *alone.*"

John glanced at Mary, playing happily with her daughter, oblivious to the others in the room.

He nodded to Alex. "Right."

"She's a beautiful child, Mary," Alex said softly, after John and Isabella had left.

Mary was euphoric. "Isn't she just," she replied, grinning broadly.

"It's a shame you won't be seeing her again."

Mary's eyes flashed as she pulled Nancy towards her.

"She's staying with me," Mary cried. "She's *mine.*"

"And how are you going to support her, Mary?" continued Alex in an even tone.

"John'll look after us, won't you John...?" Mary looked around her.

"John?" she called anxiously. "Where's John?"

Annie made to move towards her sister, but Alex stopped her.

"He's gone with Isabella, Mary," he told her. "They need to talk."

Mary shrank back clutching Nancy and realising in an instant her fate. "Don't make me go back to Billy," she begged, tears welling in her eyes. "He hates me. Annie, tell him, Billy hates me."

Annie felt herself panic at Mary's distress. "You don't have to go back to Billy, Mary," she told her, crossing quickly to her sister's side. "You can come home with me."

Mary's eyes opened wide. "You'd take me in?" she asked incredulously. "Even after all that's happened?"

Annie nodded. "Of course I'd take you in, Mary - both you and Nancy."

Mary threw her arms around Annie and this time, Alex didn't intervene.

"Come on Mary," she whispered. "I'll look after you, just like I've always done."

Mary nodded and hugged Nancy. "Can mammy come home?" she asked the child.

"Mama, 'ome," cried Nancy, kissing Mary's cheek and burying her small head into her neck.

Mary stood up and looked around the bare room. "It wasn't meant to be like this Annie," she said sadly. "Not like this."

John and Isabella Anderson walked silently by the dockside, their eyes looking out over the waters of the Forth but seeing nothing. "Why did you come?" John eventually asked, his whole body trembling in the cold wind.

"Because I love you," replied Isabella. "And I want you to come home."

John stopped and leant on the sea wall, his head in his hands. "I'm not worthy of your love, Isabella," he told her. "I'm not worthy of anybody's love."

"If you mean Mary," she responded. "You're right. She doesn't deserve to be living in an attic in Edinburgh, apart from her child."

John covered his ears. "Stop it, Isabella, *stop it.*"

Isabella gently pulled his hands from his ears. "And I don't deserve to be left alone to face the future without you."

John felt the last of his self-respect crumble. "Has her sister come for her?" he asked.

Isabella nodded. "She needs to be with her child, John, and Nancy with her mother. That can't be, as long as she's here with you."

John Anderson lifted his eyes to the clouds scuttling past in the wind. "What have I done?" he asked his God. "What have I done?"

Isabella put her hand on his shoulder and squeezed it gently. "Come home, John," she asked calmly. "Just come home with me."

John gazed at the angel before him who was his wife, and shook his head. "I loved her, Isabella," he murmured. "That hasn't changed."

Isabella felt her chin begin to tremble. "I know," she said. "I know."

"So I can't go back to Dundee," he continued. "Not ever."

Isabella felt her calmness giving way to panic as the thought of never seeing her husband again took hold of her. "Then I'll move here," she told him, more decisively than she felt. "We could make a new life for ourselves here."

John raised his eyes to meet hers. "You'd do that for me, after all that's happened?"

Isabella nodded. "My love for you has no conditions, John," she told him. "And I can't bear the thought of the rest of my life without you."

A small glimmer of hope tugged at John Anderson's heart as he took Isabella's hands in his. "Forgive me for what I've done, Isabella and I thank God for bringing you here today."

"I'll come back as soon as I can, when I've sorted a few things out and we'll begin again, John."

Her husband nodded. "Whatever you say, Isabella, whatever your say."

"Everything will be alright," she reassured him, gazing at his worried eyes. "Believe me, with God's help, we'll get through this."

They were all exhausted by the time the train pulled into the station at Dundee.

Alex carried Nancy the rest of the way home, with Mary and Annie walking wearily behind him. Back safely at Annie's tiny home, Mary put Nancy to bed while Annie made some tea for them all.

"You've been wonderful Alex," she told him, handing him his cup.

"So have you," he replied.

Annie blushed at the compliment. "I suppose I'll have Billy to deal with tomorrow, when he's released," she said. "But at least Mary's back and Nancy's happy again."

"You don't have to face it alone you know," Alex said gently. "You've got me now."

Annie felt a stillness descend on her. "Have I?" she asked, hardly daring to hope he meant it.

"Everything'll be alright, Annie," he reminded her, smiling. "Trust me, I'm a Sergeant in the Dundee Constabulary."

Annie laughed. "And I'm a Dundee weaver, home at last. Now finish your tea."

"Will you show me to the door, Annie?" asked Alex, his eyes twinkling. Annie felt herself blush scarlet under his gaze, as she opened the door into the night.

Alex stepped into the walkway and turned to face her. “Is there a chance this Dundee weaver may consent to step out with me?”

“Why Sergeant Melville,” Annie countered, feeling a surge of happiness bring the sparkle back to her eyes. “I would be honoured.”

“Aren’t the stars over William Lane just beautiful,” murmured Alex, moving Annie closer to him to see the sky.

“Are you two going to stand at that door forever?” Mary voice called out, unaware of their conversation and wrapped up as she was in the joy of seeing her child again. “Nancy’s getting a draught.”

Annie pulled the door shut behind her as Alex kissed her soundly on the lips.

Annie felt a wave of desire flow through her as she responded to his warmth.

“I’ll call in on Wednesday then, if that’s alright,” Alex whispered, returning Annie’s feet to the doorstep. “I think we’ve more to say to one another, but this isn’t the time or the place.”

Annie nodded happily. “Wednesday it is, Alex,” she smiled.

The cold grey light of Monday’s dawn filtered in through the bars of Billy’s cell where he lay shivering. He could hear the cursing and coughing of his fellow inmates and the clanking of metal keys in locks as the jailer went on his round.

Billy’s cell door swung open and banged against the stone wall.

“William Dawson,” intoned Constable MacPherson.

Billy nodded.

“Follow me.”

Billy’s head ached with lack of sleep and his legs wobbled as he stood up and followed the Constable out of the cell.

“Sergeant Melville wants a word with you,” he told Billy meaningfully, knocking on a solid brown door marked ‘Office’. “Which means only one thing…” continued Ewan McPherson, as Billy’s heart began to pound in his chest. “You’re in trouble.”

He pushed Billy through the door. “Stand up straight,” he ordered out of the corner of his mouth.

“William Dawson, Sergeant,” the Constable announced. Alex nodded silently in acknowledgement.

“Is there anything else Sergeant?”

Alex shook his head. “No, Constable, that’ll be all just now.”

Billy felt a wave of nausea wash over him as the door closed behind him.

Alex observed the change of pallor but said nothing. "Do you remember much of Saturday night, Mr Dawson?"

Billy felt the tension in his neck increase as he made his response. "I do," he managed to say.

"The charge is drunkenness and disturbance of the peace," continued Alex. "And you'll be appearing before the Procurator Fiscal…" Alex took his watch from his pocket and looked at it. "In three hours' time."

Billy's eyes remained fixed on the brass lamp on Alex's desk.

"Which means," continued Alex, "That you won't be able to report for work."

Billy was acutely aware of the implications his crime would have on his reputation at the mill and on Mr Campbell the Mill Manager in particular and tensed his muscles even more.

Sure that his message had hit home, Alex voice softened.

"You wife's back in Dundee," he told Billy. "She's reunited with her daughter and her sister and she's quite well."

The two men's eyes met.

"And before you even think of it Billy," Alex added. "I'd advise you to stay away from her."

Billy felt a surge of adrenalin force its way through the nausea.

"She's been through enough, Billy, as has Annie, and I won't see you cause them any more distress, either drunk or sober."

Billy's teeth clenched at the mention of Annie's name. "You seem very interested in their welfare, Sergeant Melville," Billy said sarcastically. "If you get my meaning."

Alex Melville stood up and walked over to Billy. "Let me tell you something," Alex began, his voice low and deliberate. "I don't like bullies and even more than that, I don't like bullies who bully women. Do you get my meaning, Mr Dawson?"

Alex Melville never took his eyes of Billy's as the words left his lips and found their mark.

Billy felt the nausea again. "I only want to see my daughter," he muttered, suddenly losing his nerve under Alex's gaze.

Alex nodded. "I'm sure Mary will agree to that, provided you behave yourself."

"Provided I behave myself," Billy whispered ironically. "Me, Billy Dawson, being told to behave himself." All at once, the tension of the last few weeks seemed to hit him and Billy began to laugh and cry at once, his whole body shaking with emotion.

Alex pushed a chair towards him and waited till the sobs subsided and

Billy had calmed down.

"I've lost everything, haven't I?" he stated bleakly, staring at nothing in particular. "My daughter, my wife, my reputation…" Billy smiled ruefully. "And now… probably my job." He looked at Alex. "It wasn't meant to be like this."

Alex went to the door of the office and ordered Constable McPherson to bring in two mugs of tea. He was sure now Billy would listen to his demands.

"It doesn't have to be like this," Alex told him. There is a way forward, if you're willing to hear me out."

Billy sat back in the chair. "I'm listening," he said warily.

Alex looked at his watch again. "Almost ten-past six," he told Billy. "If the charges against you were dropped, you could leave now and be at Baxters by seven o'clock in time to start the shift…" Alex's voice dropped. "And nobody need by any the wiser."

Billy's eyes widened. "And why would you do that for me?"

There was a knock at the door and Constable MacPherson entered with the mugs of hot tea.

He handed a cup to Billy and put the other on Alex's desk and left.

"Drink your tea, Billy," continued Alex. "There's one condition."

Billy's moment of relief was quickly replaced by a feeling of being 'on the hook' again. "And what's that, then?"

Alex sipped his tea before replying. "You stay away from Annie," he said bluntly. "Forever."

Billy let the words sink in to his consciousness. His eyes narrowed, as understanding dawned. "So that's it," he said. "Annie… you want Annie."

"And I'll have her too," replied Alex. "The hard way… or the easy way."

"You're a clever man, Sergeant Melville," he told Alex. "But so's Annie and she's not easily fooled."

"Then you agree?" Alex continued, ignoring Billy's comment.

Reluctantly, Billy nodded. "I agree."

"Constable MacPherson," Alex called out. "Through here, please."

The Constable's head leaned through the door opening. "Yes, Sergeant?"

"Mr Dawson's released without charge, Constable. Give him his belongings and see him on his way."

Constable MacPherson's eyes questioned his Sergeant.

"Quickly now, Constable," Billy urged. "Mr Dawson's going to be late for his work."

The policeman swung the door wider in obedience. "This way, Mr Dawson," he indicated smartly.

The two men faced one another silently for a few seconds, each aware of the other's power. Billy turned on his heel and quickly left the room.

Alex walked to the window and stood there till he saw Billy cross the yard and go through the iron gate out into Bell Street.

Constable MacPherson's voice cut through his thoughts. "Mr Dawson's off the premises, Sergeant. Is there anything else you'll be wanting before I draw up the charge sheet for the Fiscal?

Alex turned to meet his gaze. "No, Constable MacPherson, nothing. Except, maybe the duty roster for the week. I've a very important appointment to keep… on Wednesday.

THE END

Lightning Source UK Ltd.
Milton Keynes UK
UKHW022020291021
393062UK00011B/1919

9 780993 133206